A LOCAL MATTER

A LOCAL MATTER
A Murder Case from the Notes of George Howard, Secretary to Lord Alfred Tigraines

JOHN McGREW BENNETT

Walker and Company
New York

Copyright © 1985 by John McGrew Bennett

All rights reserved. No part of this book may be
reproduced or transmitted in any form or by any
means, electric or mechanical, including photocopying,
recording, or by any information storage and retrieval
system, without permission in writing from the Publisher.

All the characters and events portrayed in this story
are fictitious.

First published in the United States of America
in 1985 by the Walker Publishing Company, Inc.

Published simultaneously in Canada by John Wiley & Sons
Canada, Limited, Rexdale, Ontario.

Library of Congress Cataloging in Publication Data

Bennett, John McGrew.
  A local matter.

  I. Title.
PS3552.E54735L6   1985   813'.54   84-15330
ISBN 0-8027-5603-4

Printed in the United States of America

  10   9   8   7   6   5   4   3   2   1

To my parents and the friend on their wall.

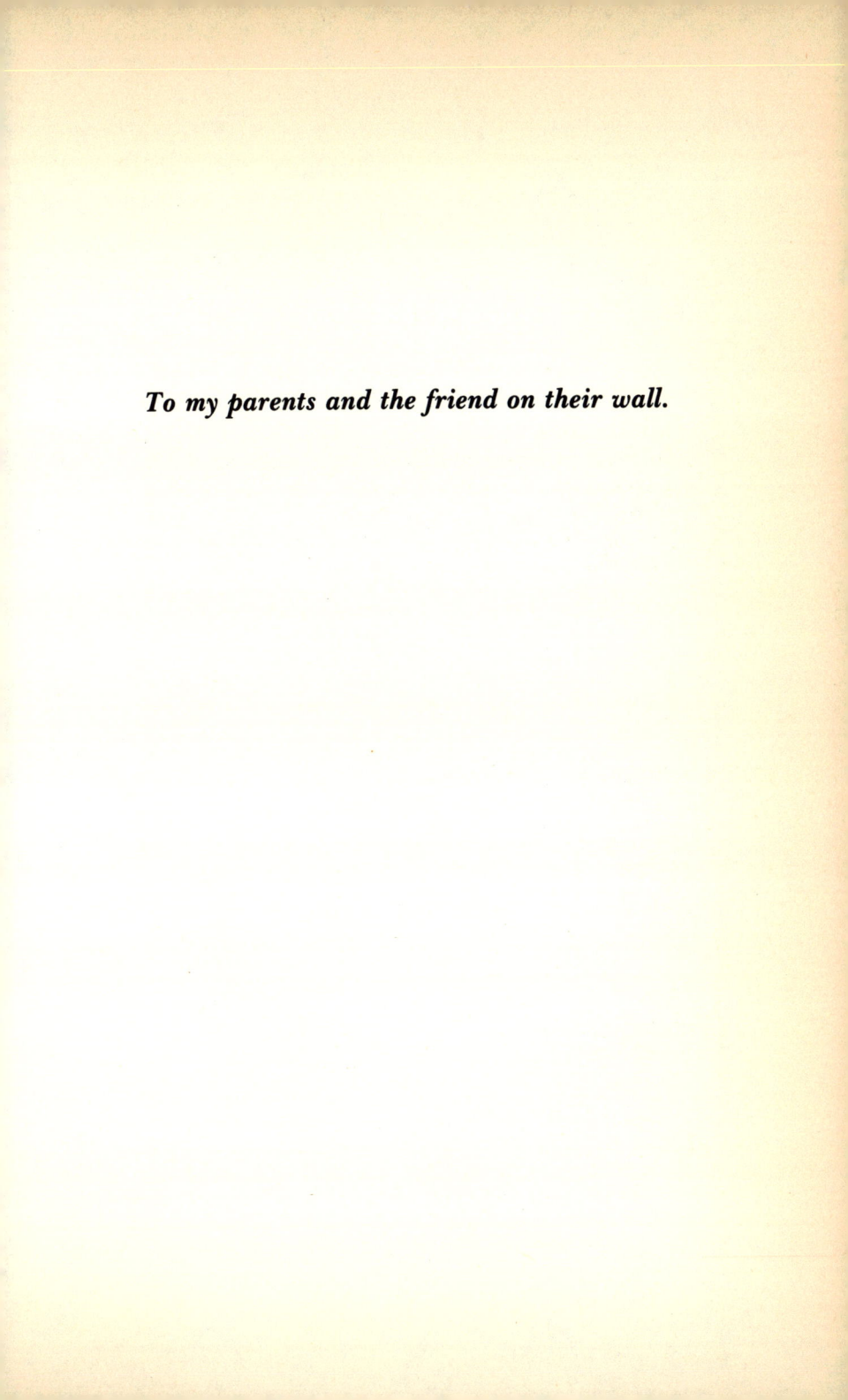

ACKNOWLEDGMENTS

An important contribution to this book was made by the editors Sara Ann Freed and Ruth Cavin who, when the manuscript was unfinished, said to look for a face in a market, visit a place in the night, and find what was written on stone.

Preface

George Howard, who was my great-uncle, left America in his youth, years before what was called the Great War. No one knew where he was going or what he might have been looking for; but for a while he was on a Dutch trading vessel that traveled the Andaman Sea. A fading postcard he sent from Siam shows a temple entangled in vines. Another one, from India, has a picture of a jeweled elephant. And it was in India, on the road to Kabul, that my great-uncle met Lord Tigraines, whose secretary he would become.

None of this meant very much to his family, to whom he remained a black sheep; but when he returned to America after the Second World War, it appeared that he had become a man of some substance.

I remember the wonder I felt when my parents took me to visit him in New York. In the narrow hallway inside his door, he had a small Persian chest that was inlaid with ivory and gems. He had Indian carpets, Chinese porcelain, and a figure from an Egyptian tomb. What he seemed to prize most, however, was a painting of a man in a turban who I thought at first was a sheik.

My great-uncle must have seen me stare at this painting, for he came over and put a hand on my shoulder, as the old often do with the young. "Do you like the painting?" he asked, his voice with an accent strange to me, neither English nor American.

"Yes," I said, but I was not sure that I did. The face in the painting had dark, piercing eyes that would haunt me for years afterward.

"That is Lord Tigraines," said my great-uncle, as if the painting and the man were the same.

"Was Lord Tigraines an Arabian?" I asked.

"He was an Englishman," my great-uncle said. "He was the greatest of all Englishmen and may have been the greatest man in the world. The reason you see him dressed that way is that he once went to Mecca. That was the disguise he used there."

My great-uncle died shortly after this meeting, and in his will it was said that the painting should be returned to the Tigraines estate. I do not know why no one ever did so. Perhaps it was too difficult to mail and too expensive to deliver in person, but it remained along with other objects in the attic of my parents' home. Years later, when I discovered it there, I found that it was already wrapped and had a note about the will attached to it. It was as though it had always been waiting for this moment when I was leaving for England and would be able to take it with me.

I did not know if there would be anyone who would care about such a thing then; but shortly after my arrival in London, I explained about the painting in a letter that I sent to Lord Tigraines' heirs, addressed to the town of Marley where he had lived.

At first I thought it might take a long time for such heirs even to be located, but no more than three days could have passed before an answer arrived in the mail. Written on violet-trimmed stationery with a coat of arms at the top, the reply I received had been signed by a woman named Ethel McNaught.

"You must come to Longmoor at once," said this letter. "I remember the painting, and I remember your great-uncle. I am old, and so you must not delay."

Longmoor, as it turned out, was the name of Lord Tigraines' old estate, and Ethel McNaught was actually Lady Ethel. A niece of the late Lord Tigraines, she did not live in the great house itself; it had become something of a museum. Instead she occupied the former gardener's cottage, which was sufficiently modernized not to depend on the dwindling forests for fuel.

"So you are Mr. Howard's grandnephew," she said when I arrived at her door with the painting. "Do you know, you must be the same age that he was the first time we met? That was in Ireland, and it was a long time ago. I remember I was out with the sheep when he drove up with Uncle Alfred. Uncle Tiger I used to call him."

"You called my great-uncle that?" I asked her.

"No," she said, "that was what I called Lord Tigraines. Your great-uncle was always Mr. Howard. Were you ever told that you look a great deal like him?"

Lady Ethel took me into the cottage where she insisted I share with her the herb tea that she claimed was the secret of health. Health was certainly one thing she had, but something else, even more striking then, was the remarkable way that she looked. The beauty she must have had in her youth, instead of fading, had become more intense, like that of a flower that has been pressed in a book.

"Did you know my great-uncle well?" I asked her.

"I knew him very well," she told me. "He was Lord Tigraines' secretary, of course; but in a way he was much more than that. They were friends. They often traveled together. They even shared, after I was orphaned, in the task of bringing me up."

By then the painting was unwrapped, and I realized that if I looked like my great-uncle, Lady Ethel looked like her relative, too. She had the same piercing eyes, though in a woman's face they seemed softer. "Yes," she said, "that is just how he looked. Once, when I was a little girl, Mr. Howard and my governess said that my uncle wanted to speak to me about something I had done wrong. I went to the library, but instead of seeing my uncle, I saw this Arab with a turban and sword. He was not frightening, only strangely majestic. He read to me a wonderful story about a man who was called Ahikar and who made a rope out of sand."

I explained again, as I had in the letter, that I was sorry it had taken so long to carry out my great-uncle's instructions to return the painting to the estate. Lady Ethel smiled. "Do you know," she said, "you almost talk like him, too? But you must not worry about the painting. I told Mr. Howard on the day that he left that it would always be his, if he liked. He said, though, just as you have told me, that he would ask for its return in his will. He knew it might take a long time, but he was sure it would come back some day. And when it did, if someone brought it in person, he wanted that person to be shown something. He wanted me to show that person the chest."

"The chest?" I asked.

"His chest of treasures," she said. "But it is not here. It is up at the house, and it is too late to go there today. Have you arranged yet for a place to stay?"

"I am staying at the Green Fox," I replied.

"Of course," she said. "That is perfect for you. But tomorrow you must come back, and then I will take you up to the house."

The next day, when we went to the house, Lady Ethel showed me the chest. It was not, perhaps, a treasure chest in the sense I had been led to expect. Actually, it was an old steamer trunk that had possibly belonged to my great-uncle from the time when he first went away. Placed now beneath one of the windows in the little upstairs room where he had worked, the trunk contained not jewels but papers. In one stack were household inventories, menus for different occasions, and even the cellar wine lists. In another were more personal matters, such as letters my great-uncle had received and clippings from English newspapers. But the third and by far largest stack was the one of most interest to me, for in it were travel diaries, notebooks, and accounts of his life with the lord.

Lady Ethel said she had already attempted to read one of these accounts herself, but it was written in a kind of shorthand that she found difficult to decipher. I, too, had difficulty at first, until I got help from someone in London who was acquainted with mirror-writing. After that it was all very simple, and the result was what you will read here.

In rendering my great-uncle's shorthand, I have been forced to supply articles, pronouns, and even an occasional verb. Otherwise it is all as he wrote it, and the only other change is in the title. My great-uncle entitled his work "Nimrod," which did not seem right to me; and so I have called it "A Local Matter." This phrasing appears in the text and describes the central problem, a murder, which agitated the nearby town long ago.

As will be seen, most of the events take place in the year 1914, but they begin the December before, as Lord Tigraines and my great-uncle discuss whether a new arrival in Marley might be someone they should get to know. Though my great-uncle says Lord Tigraines rarely worked on a case, it appears that in the field of detection, as in many others, Lord Tigraines was unmatched.

One

*L*ord Tigraines once made the comment that no guest was more likely to bore than one the world thought a genius. Over the years we had a number of proofs of this rather humorous maxim, but nevertheless he was always willing to put it to the test once again. One day at the end of 1913, when we were preparing for the New Year's banquet, his lordship said to me: "George, I understand the Redland place has been sold."

"Yes, I heard the same thing," I told him. "The new owner is a man named Hart, I believe."

"Sir James Hart, the archaeologist?" he asked.

"I am not sure," I answered. "Would you like me to make inquiries?"

"By all means," he said, "but make them discreetly. If it is Sir James, I think we might become friends."

As it turned out, there was no need for discretion, nor even to make inquiries. When I went to the post office that morning, Sir James Hart was the main topic of discussion among the townspeople there. One of these people, who happened to be the vicar, even appeared incensed at the idea that an apostate had moved in among us.

"Archaeology is one thing," said the vicar, "but it is quite another when obscene pagan idols are dug up for purposes of worship."

I made no comment, but merely purchased some stamps, after which I crossed the street to the bookstore where two of Sir James' recent books were in prominent window display. The one entitled *The Triumph of Nimrod* was already in his lordship's library. The other one, *The Descent of Ishtar*, must have been what had upset the vicar. I would not have called the jacket picture obscene, but it did depict a female idol in a state of partial nakedness.

"What did you find out?" asked his lordship, when I returned with the second book in brown paper.

I handed him the package, and he unwrapped it at once. "Only that you were right," I told him. "Our new neighbor is Sir James Hart himself."

"Then we will invite him here," said Lord Tigraines. "The New Year's banquet ought to be the right time."

"But the vicar will be coming," I said.

"Yes, so he will," said his lordship. "Are you thinking that might cause difficulties?"

"Mr. Halliday," I explained, "does not like what he calls obscene pagan idols."

"In that event, George," said his lordship. "Sir James should have a chance to defend them. Is the gentleman married, do you happen to know?"

"All the talk was about him," I said. "I did not hear if there was a Lady Hart."

"Then," said his lordship, "take the invitation in person. If you find there is a wife, please assure her that she will be welcome, too."

It was rare for Lord Tigraines to take such interest in a neighbor, and the reason for it on this occasion was that he was something of an archaeologist himself. As is well known, he had once had involvement with an important excavation in Egypt. More recently, with my help and the gardener's, he had been exploring an underground vault, not far from the Roman road on his land.

In order to get to the Redland estate, I had to pass once

again through the town, where the curious were now gathered outside the bookstore. It was fortunate, I said to myself, that I had purchased the book when I had, for it seemed likely that in a short time the whole stack of copies would be sold. Also I wondered if Sir James himself might not have been besieged by then, but there was no such crowd outside his house. Turning in at the gate, I drove up the bumpy, overgrown path that looked as though it had never before felt the wheels of a modern automobile.

It was not necessary for me to announce myself, nor even to get out of the car. On my arrival I was greeted by two dogs whose barking seemed loud enough to be heard all the way back to town. One of the dogs leaped at the hood, while the other, half the height of a man, scratched at the door I kept closed.

The gentleman who emerged from the house had something almost patriarchal in his lean, bearded face. He was not an old man, but his brow was so furrowed, and his skin so deeply weathered and lined, that he looked as the mighty Nimrod himself might have looked in his days on the sand. Even his clothes, though they seemed to be new, were not those of the English countryside. They were the clothes of a traveler of deserts, and of a man careless of what others might think. He called off the dogs with a high, chirping sound, but the dogs did not retreat very far. Squatting as if ready to spring, they kept growling all the time I was there.

"I must inform you, sir," the man said to me, "that if you are a commercial agent, I have no interest in what you have to sell."

"Are you Sir James Hart?" I asked.

"I am," he said.

"Then on behalf of my employer," I told him, "I am here to invite you to the New Year's banquet at Longmoor."

"And what is Longmoor?" he asked.

"It is the estate of Lord Tigraines," I said.

"Lord Tigraines," said Sir James, "must be the lord of the local manor."

"He may be that when he is here," I explained, "but he is also a man of the world. I think, in fact, you will find that his interests are similar to your own. Lord Tigraines financed the Compson expedition in Egypt. You must have heard of it, since it was the one that uncovered the black statue of Isis that was recently stolen from its museum."

"Oh, yes," he said for the first time with a smile, "so often it is the thefts, not the discoveries, that our modern world celebrates. If a man is truly anxious for fame, he should be a murderer or a thief."

"I will tell his lordship you said that," I told him. "He is someone who also enjoys wit."

When I returned to Longmoor, I not only told Lord Tigraines about this, but expressed the opinion that Sir James was something of an eccentric. I described the dogs, the general state of the grounds, and the appearance of the archaeologist himself. From the way the man dressed, I said, it had not been necessary to ask if he was married.

"Or had a valet," added his lordship.

"No, certainly not," I said.

"Well," said Lord Tigraines with a sigh, "at least he has an interesting mind. We can look forward to his conversation, if not to the cut of his clothes."

Two

The New Year's banquet started, as usual, at three with the arrival of the vicar and his wife. I took their coats, which were dripping with rain, and showed them into the main drawing room. "Are we the first?" Mr. Halliday asked, as his lordship rose to shake their hands.

"You are indeed," said Lord Tigraines, "and in this weather you may well be the last."

"I would hardly think that," said the vicar. "This is the social event of the year. I understand even Sir James Hart is coming."

The Hallidays were provided with drinks, a hot cider spiced with cinnamon, and they took seats on the couch by the fire. "Are you acquainted with Sir James?" asked his lordship.

"I have not met him personally," the vicar responded. "So far he has not come to church. But I know his reputation, of course."

Lord Tigraines, with a glance at me, nodded. "As a man of the church," said his lordship, "you naturally would have some interest in his archaeological work."

"Very much so," Mr. Halliday said. "The church is always greatly concerned with any light thrown on Biblical texts. His book on Nimrod might not be one that I would want read in our Sunday school, but no one has ever done more to bring that ancient figure to life. My wife has even found merit in his treatment of the goddess Ishtar. She thinks our own Christian traditions ignore the female principle."

Mrs. Halliday, in her dignified way, had begun elaborating on this when I was called to the door once again. The new guests were Mr. and Mrs. Alexander, after whom came the Ravenwoods, the Shakespeares, and the Simpsons from nearby Whitcross. Both the Simpsons and Shakespeares had children for whom his lordship had provided gifts. While these children opened their packages, another group of people arrived. Sir James was not among them, however, and so I asked his lordship if the meal should be delayed.

"I see no reason for that," he told me. "If he is late, it is his fault, not ours."

During the first course, which was his lordship's favorite lentil soup, the guests were all asked for predictions of what would happen in the new year. Dr. Simpson, who was his lordship's physician, predicted that a royal family in Europe would be cursed by the arrival of twins. "They will be identical in all respects," said the doctor, "and mixed up from the moment of birth. Finally, since no one knows which is older, a council of state will be called. After weeks of deliberation, it will be decided that one boy must die. He will be strangled in secret by the chancellor, who is the most respected man in the land."

"That is completely absurd," said his lordship. "Let me remind you that this is nineteen-fourteen. Does no one have a happier prediction?"

Thomas Ravenwood, who was our town's constable, did have a more pleasant prediction. "I predict a year without crime," he told us. "There will be no more Jack the Rippers, no more murders, and no more robberies of banks. People in the city of London will be able to go out and leave their doors open. When money is found on the street, it will be returned to its rightful owners."

"That will certainly be a happy world," said his lordship,

"but it will also put you out of work. What new task will you turn your hand to?"

"There will still be work for me," Ravenwood said. "After all, there are these new motorcars, and there are children and dogs that get lost, which are the only problems we have here anyway."

"And thank goodness for that," said Amanda Shakespeare. "Would it not be absolutely awful if we had to live in London or over in the United States? Do you know, I heard that in California there are towns where men are killed every day? People shoot them on the street."

"That may have happened in the gold rush," said Lord Tigraines, "but I think you will find that America is more civilized now. Our friend George here is American, and somehow he survived being shot. I doubt that even an Indian attacked him."

"His lordship is right," I agreed. "I have never been to California, but I hear the main problem there is earthquakes."

"Exactly," his lordship said, "and now, George, it is time for you to make your prediction."

"My prediction is the same as last year's," I told them. "There will probably be a few local matters that seem important to us here, but otherwise very little will happen."

"Apparently you reject then," said his lordship, "both this double birth of kings and that all crime will come to a stop."

"I most certainly do," I responded, "I reject anything dramatic except a new play by Mr. Shaw."

"Mr. Maugham might not be pleased to hear that," said Lord Tigraines, "but at least everyone here can see why I value this secretary of mine. Not only does he predict a dull year; he even looks forward to it. Let us hope, for the world's sake, he is right, though I cannot be so certain myself. It seems to me that the borders of Europe could be shaken by an earthquake themselves."

"Do not tell me you are saying that there might be a war,"

said Sam Shakespeare. "Who would be fool enough to start one?"

"That I will leave to the vicar," said his lordship, "since his prediction is next anyway."

The vicar did not have a prediction. All he did was to offer a prayer for peace and goodwill among men, after which Mrs. Halliday made the comment that there would never be peace in the world until women held positions of power.

There had still been no sign of Sir James, and his absence did not go unnoticed. When the person who took away our soup plates wished to know if the second course of green salad should be set at the empty place next to mine, my answer was yes, that one guest was delayed, but that he might well arrive at any moment.

"I assume," Amanda Shakespeare said then, "that you are speaking of the man with the dogs who occupies the old house next to ours."

"That is right, you must be friends," said his lordship. "I completely forgot that Sir James is living next to your own charming place."

"He lives next to us, but we are not friends," answered the lady. "I told Sam when the man first moved in that he should go and invite him for tea, but Sam was hardly inside the gate when those dogs chased him away. It seems unlikely, from what we know now, that Sir James would have wanted tea anyway. He appears to prefer stronger drink."

"Please, Amanda, you should not say that," said Sam. "We have no proof that our neighbor is a drinker."

"We hear the noise. That is enough," said his wife. "He and that woman are up half the night, yelling and screaming at each other."

"Is Sir James married then?" asked Lord Tigraines. "George assured me that from the way the man dressed he would have to be a bachelor."

Amanda Shakespeare, with a smile, cast a superior glance

in my direction. "I know nothing of the way he dresses," she said. "I know only the way he behaves, and his behavior, believe me, is disgraceful. I think, from the way she was once screaming, that the woman was actually struck."

"Well, George, what do you say to that?" asked his lordship. "Do you think your powers of deduction have slipped?"

"Very possibly they have," I admitted. "I never considered that he might be like Socrates and married to a woman who is a shrew. A wife like that would explain the state of his clothing as well as the screams in the night."

"Not to mention the drinking," said his lordship, "since Socrates was not unknown for that. As I see it, the only problem we have now is what to do if Sir James brings this Xanthippe with him. We will have to set another place at the table."

"That will not be necessary," I said. "If he comes, and does bring a wife, I will give up my own place to her."

"That would be noble," said his lordship, "but I detect something of a challenge in it. You do not really believe that the man is going to come with a wife."

"No, I do not," I explained. "If there were a wife, she would have been seen in town."

It was unusual for Lord Tigraines to engage in common gossip like this, but he was, along with other pursuits, interested in human nature. The vicar, the constable, and the doctor appeared equally interested; only the member of the legal profession, Sam Shakespeare, seemed at all uncomfortable.

"You must pardon Amanda," Sam said, "but I have told her several times that the voices we heard could have come from a Gramophone record."

"Do you mean to say," asked his lordship, "that the voices could have been violins?"

"Not that," said Sam. "They were voices. But I went to an opera in London where the screaming was almost the same."

"Was it singing?" his lordship asked. "Was there music?"

Amanda Shakespeare seemed about to deny this, but she

stopped when it was announced that the man we were talking about had arrived.

Sir James was alone, just as I had predicted, but nevertheless I did feel some surprise when he settled down in the seat at my side. His hair was neat, his beard carefully trimmed, and his clothing sufficiently formal for a ceremony of investiture. Except for the rain that had muddied his shoes, as well as caused his starched collar to bend, he might have been as elegant as any other man in the room.

"We have just been talking about you, Sir James," Amanda Shakespeare said from across the table. "My husband Sam and I are your neighbors and have wanted to have you over to tea."

"And I was also telling his lordship," said the vicar, "that I have regretted not seeing you in church. I am sure that with the work you have done you could make a valuable contribution to our understanding of some of the texts."

"You are flattering me," said Sir James, his voice no longer as rough as it had been on that day we first met. "I am only a digger in sand who on occasion has had the good fortune to find a few carvings in stone."

"You put it too modestly," said the vicar. "After all, there are also your books."

"Have you read my books?" asked Sir James.

"I have not, but my wife has," said the vicar. "If your books have done nothing more, they have made her generation aware that there was a time when women were actually worshiped."

"Have they ever stopped being worshiped?" asked his lordship in a comment that brought this discussion to a fitting end.

One disappointment to me was that no one, not even the constable, was to probe Sir James on the question of whether he had a Gramophone. He was asked at one point by his lordship if he would like to make a prediction for the year, but he declined, saying even the past was difficult for him to read.

Altogether, as the vicar had said, he was apparently a modest gentleman, and he gave no sign either of being a genius or of engaging in the sort of behavior that the Shakespeares had heard in the night. Not only, when wine and brandy were served, did he refrain from drinking even one glass, but so eager to please did he seem that Amanda Shakespeare was completely won over. When the company finally broke up, the Shakespeares drove him home in their car.

Three

*L*ord Tigraines was rarely content to stay very long at Longmoor. Shortly after the New Year's banquet, he went to visit his sister in Ireland and then to London where he planned to remain at least until the middle of June. I joined him in March, at which time there were rumors all over London that he would be offered a cabinet post. His lordship, however, denied that either then or at any time in the future would he consider accepting such a position. His own explanation for the fact that so many politicians came to call was that they had a common interest in cards.

Of course, there were also other matters that were occupying him then. He had missed the theater in the fall and had to catch up on all the new plays, including the one entitled *Lord Dilettante* that had been based (there seemed no doubt of this) on his lordship's adventures in Spain. Lord Tigraines, when he returned from this play, was to claim that he saw no resemblance between himself and the fictional hero who solved the mystery of the theft of some diamonds, which in the end proved to be paste. "The mystery was the same," Lord Tigraines admitted, "but I am sure I was never as pompous as that insufferable man on the stage. Have you ever known me to drop names as he did? Have I ever withheld evidence to make the police seem more foolish than they are?"

"I have known you to withhold your theories," I told him, "and sometimes that has made me feel foolish, too."

His lordship frowned. "My brain is slow," he responded. "I am never able to make those quick leaps of judgment that someone with a mind like yours can. I need facts, and then more and more facts, before a theory falls into place."

"And you are always right," I said. "That is the trouble. That is what makes it so maddening."

I had not, at that point, seen the play; but when I went to a matinee the next week, the audience gasped, as I had once gasped myself, when the lord brought down the mallet, smashing the worthless gems of Madrid. Lord Tigraines was certainly right, however, about the character of the man on the stage. Not only was he a pompous name-dropper, forever saying, "As I said to the Queen" or "As I told Bertie once," but he was also a man who chased women, which was something Lord Tigraines never did. There were times, perhaps, when there were ladies, as there was Lady Catherine in London right then, who may have thought they could take the place of the bride whom his lordship had lost in his youth. But Lord Tigraines, though not a religious man, believed he had married once for all time. Each morning, when he was living at Longmoor, he would pause on his way down to breakfast to gaze at that dark, oval face that had been painted by a Russian in France. "He was a madman," his lordship said of this painter. "But he caught my wife's face perfectly. When I see that painting, I see her."

The time would come with almost every lady when she realized she could not compete with a ghost. Once this happened, there might still be flirtation. The lady might even become more bold, but her visits would be far less frequent, and in the company of other ladies and men.

This was the stage reached by Lady Catherine after little more than a month, and I noticed it seemed to sadden his lordship more than it ever had in the past. On afternoons when he might have been out riding, I would find him instead with a book, and he started spending his evenings at home even when there were no visitors. We were both at home on that evening in May when our friend from the country appeared.

"I know I am intruding," said Sam Shakespeare, as I was taking his coat at the door. "Lord Tigraines is not the sort of person whom one should drop in on like this."

"On the contrary," I told him, "I am sure his lordship will be pleased to see you."

The solicitor was both out of breath and in a state of nervous agitation. "Tell his lordship," he said, "that I just arrived in London tonight and have come straight to him from the station. It is not for myself, you understand. It is for the girl who has been accused of the murder."

"The murder?" I asked.

"Have you not heard?" said Sam. "The news is all over the evening papers. Sir James Hart was found dead this morning."

Lord Tigraines, who had been in his study, had come out and was standing in the hall. "Please go out and get a paper," he told me, "and see that Sam's things are brought in from his cab. When you get back, we will want you to join us."

When I got back, and the suitcase was upstairs, I found that Sam had already recounted his version of what had occurred. He and his lordship were sitting in silence, with glasses of brandy in their hands. "It is certainly a distressing event," Lord Tigraines said as I entered the room. "What does the newspaper have to say about it?"

I showed him the headline, "Famous Archaeologist Dead," and then, when I had poured my own brandy, I proceeded to read the article out loud. This is what it said:

> Sir James Hart, the well-known Assyriologist and author, was found dead in his country home, an apparent victim of poisoning. Sir James lived alone in the house, and the local constable, Thomas Ravenwood, has wasted no time in arresting the young woman who worked as his housekeeper.
>
> This was not the first time that Sir James had

faced violence, since in the course of his career he was twice kidnapped by brigands and once nearly drowned at sea. What seems surprising, however, is that the latest incident, and the most unfortunate, occurred in what is often considered one of England's most picturesque towns.

Sir James moved to the village of Marley shortly after returning to England from a convalescence in France. There had been a time, after the near drowning, when he was not expected to live. But he survived, both to the surprise of his doctors and to the delight of the scholarly world. Sir James' last book, *The Descent of Ishtar*, has been praised as a fitting successor to the author's earlier *The Triumph of Nimrod*.

"That hardly gives us very much information," his lordship said when I was through. "But nevertheless it has its interesting points. Sir James had three encounters with death before the final one at Redland itself."

"Do you mean to suggest that there might be a connection?" I asked. "Do you think those brigands, whoever they might have been, could have followed him all the way back to England?"

"The reverse has happened," his lordship replied. "Take the famous case of Julius Caesar. He was held for ransom by pirates, and when freed he took the precaution of tracking them down and having them put to death. Otherwise, had they caught him again, the pirates might have done the work of the senate before history was ready for it."

"You mean stabbed him?" I asked.

"Yes," said his lordship. "And in the case of Sir James we find that he was kidnapped a second time. It will be interesting to learn both the circumstances of these kidnappings and how the ransoms were paid."

"And then there was the near drowning," I told him.

"Yes, there was that, too," he said. "Altogether I think these events have given us a good deal to ponder."

"But what of the housekeeper?" I asked. "The paper says she has already been arrested."

"She was a new employee," said his lordship. "I suppose you remember the daughter of our gardener Fred Quint?"

"Of course I do," I answered. "Susan Quint. She used to live with her father in his cottage."

"Until she ran off," said Lord Tigraines, "which I believe had something to do with you."

"I would hardly say that," I told him. "It is true that I took her to a performance by those actors who came into town, but the whole staff was there with us. If you remember, it was even your idea."

"So it was," said his lordship. "But the thing neither of us knew then was that Susan was a girl of ambition. We did not realize that after seeing one performance she would run off to go on the stage. You say the whole staff was there with you, but her father did not go. He must have had some sort of warning since his wife, Susan's mother, had done the same thing years before. The mother, too, had wanted to be an actress, but she was killed in a train accident before she could join a company."

"Yes," I said, "but go on about Susan. And what does she have to do with what happened to Sir James?"

It was Sam Shakespeare who answered this question: "Susan Quint—she calls herself Quintleigh now—was working as Sir James' housekeeper. She is the one who is under arrest."

Four

"It was good of his lordship to let you come," said Sam Shakespeare as he and I were on a train the next day. Trees and houses flashed by the windows. A little river was there an instant and gone, and then the train slowed as it approached a station. I could tell from the expression on Sam's face that, although he was pretending to be pleased that Lord Tigraines had let me go back with him, he was disappointed that his lordship had not been able to accompany us.

When the train stopped, a conductor opened the door for a lady in a feathered hat to get in. She sat down, removed the pins from her hat, and placed it on the seat beside her. I was about to ask if it would not be better to put the hat on the rack above her, when the train, with a jolt, started forward. No longer did there seem any danger that someone else would come in and sit on the hat by mistake.

"What was really good," I said to Sam, "was that you came all the way to see us. Not many solicitors would do that, and particularly not when there is little hope of a fee."

"No, there is certainly not much hope of that," Sam agreed. "But a fee is not what I look for. What I want is to prove the girl innocent, and I was hoping his lordship would, too."

"His lordship does," I said. "We could see that last night. When we talked of the case, he already had several ideas."

"But what do they all mean?" Sam asked. "What difference does it make that Julius Caesar might have put some pirates to death? How can that help this young woman who now faces the gallows herself?"

"It is the way his lordship's mind works," I said. "He sees not only the present but the past."

We rode for some distance in silence while the lady in the compartment with us kept glancing from Sam's face to mine. Because the coat she was wearing was black, I had the thought that she was probably a widow on her way to visit a son or daughter somewhere. I thought, too, that something we had said had aroused her interest in some way. But by the time our conversation resumed, the lady had ceased giving us glances and was adjusting the feathers on her hat.

"Could his lordship have been offended," Sam asked, "when I told him that I would like fish for breakfast?"

"His lordship may have been surprised," I said, "but I doubt that he was actually offended. Did he give that impression to you?"

"Well," said Sam, "he did speak rather strongly. He said he would not allow such food in his house."

"And that is right," I said. "He will not. Even I, since I have been in his employ, have never eaten the flesh of a creature that ever swam or crawled on the earth."

"That is really extraordinary," Sam said. "I knew his lordship was like that at the banquets, but I thought for breakfast he might at least have a fish."

"If you thought that," I told him, "then you do not know his lordship. Lord Tigraines would no more eat a fish than Susan Quint would have poisoned Sir James."

"Bravo," said the lady across from us. "I was sure, when I first heard you talking, that it was about that archaeologist's murder. Is Lord Tigraines going to work on the case?"

"His lordship," I explained to the lady, "rarely works on a case. Human nature and history are his interests, as is the protection of the innocent. He will contribute, but will not intervene unless a serious miscarriage of justice forces him to take a hand."

The lady nodded, as if she knew all about this. "I met Lord Tigraines once," she said. "My late husband was a teacher of Greek, and on our honeymoon in Athens he pointed to a young man with a book who was sitting on the Acropolis steps. 'That young Diogenes,' he said, 'was my student. Come, let me introduce you.' We went over to the young man, and my husband said: 'My dear, this is Lord Tiger. My lord, I would like you to meet my wife.'"

"Your husband called him Lord Tiger?" I asked.

"That was his nickname," she said. "I am sure, in the years since, he has changed. But at that time he was the sweetest young man. He even told us that when we got back to England we should visit him at his estate."

"Did you?" I asked.

"We stopped once," she said, "but unfortunately he was away. It was the year he made his journey to Mecca."

When I heard that, I wished his lordship were there, for I knew how pleased he would have been to have met this person from the past. The lady got off at West Macott and was met, as I had surmised, by a daughter who must have looked very much like her mother on that day in Athens years before. "If you mention me to Lord Tigraines," said the lady, just before she closed the compartment door, "please tell him my late husband said once that he was the best student he ever had."

Then she was gone. The feathered hat and black coat disappeared with the daughter into the station. Sam Shakespeare and I, left alone, went back to our talk of the crime.

Five

"Why not begin at the beginning," I said, "and tell me what you told his lordship last night? How did it happen that Susan Quint found employment with Sir James?"

The coach swayed as it went around a bend in the tracks, and Sam Shakespeare, who was lighting his pipe, sucked out the flame on the match. "Lord Tigraines never asked that," he said, as he lit a fresh match and held it carefully over the bowl. "In a way, too, I was glad he did not, since it is not a story I like to tell. As you know, Susan wanted to be an actress, but that is not the easiest of professions. It seems that the troupe she ran off to join never really took her very far. She performed for a while in their tent, and then, when the troupe was forced to disband, she went in a different direction. Is it necessary, do you think, for me to give you all the details?"

"You are the solicitor, not I," I told him. "If there is something you know in confidence—"

"That is not the problem," he said. "It is just that Susan herself has said very little, and most of what I know is mere rumor. Such hearsay I do not like to repeat."

"I can assure you," I said, "that both his lordship and I will do our utmost to respect privacy, and particularly when that may pertain to the honor and reputation of a lady."

Sam drew on his pipe for a moment, then exhaled a thick

cloud of smoke. "I am afraid, George," he said, "that this young lady's reputation is beyond even his lordship's power to protect it. The rumor is that the theatrical troupe involved its women members in prostitution."

"But not Susan," I said.

"Well, no, perhaps not," Sam said. "But then there is another matter. Susan became attached to a young man. Let us say, for Susan's sake, that it was an entirely innocent flirtation. Nevertheless, when the troupe disbanded, this young man was to run off both with Susan and with the cashbox filled with receipts. They were caught and were both put in jail, though Susan in time was released when the young man took the blame on himself."

"He was honorable at least in that then," I said.

"Yes," said Sam, "but you know how young women are. Such honor, even coming from a thief, serves only to increase the attachment. She got a job in a place where she was close enough to visit him everyday. Then he escaped, and she disappeared with him. Certain objects, possibly of some value, were found missing from the house where she lived."

"And yet," I said, "you told me this was mere rumor."

"It is rumor to be sure," Sam replied, "but there may be more to it than that. Even before Susan came back to Marley, there was talk that the police were alerted. You know Ravenwood. He is like you and me. He would never start the rumor himself. But there was a man in town asking questions. People thought he might be from Scotland Yard."

"And then what happened?" I asked when he paused. "How did this bring Susan to work for Sir James?"

"I am coming to that," Sam said. "Susan was desperate, you see. When she came back to town, she did not want to burden her father. She felt too much shame to do that, and so she came to us looking for work. In the past, when my wife had small chores, she would give them to the village girls. Susan knew how to take care of a house, and that was why my wife suggested that she go to work for Sir James."

"You mean you sent her to live with that man all alone?" I asked.

"No," said Sam, "she was there only in the daytime, and after all, we would be very close."

"But what about all the shouting?" I asked.

"That had stopped," Sam said. "We heard it on one or two nights, and afterwards everything was all right. We did worry a little about the dogs, but Sir James himself seemed so pleasant and was a man of such accomplishment, that we thought there was little to fear."

It would have been hard for a man to look more chagrined than Sam Shakespeare did at that moment. Even the killer, responsible for the crime, would have been unlikely to have felt greater guilt than was written on that sensitive brow. Sam turned his face to the window, where outside, in the freedom of a field, a lone cow sadly munched at the grass.

"You must not blame yourself," I told him. "What you did was only for Susan's good."

"Yes," he said, "but as you say, we had warning. We had heard those shouts in the night and we also knew, though it was only a rumor, that Susan had been in trouble before."

A thought struck me as it might have struck Lord Tigraines, if his lordship had been in my place. "And what if that is the answer?" I said. "What if the murder was committed by that young man?"

"Do you mean," said Sam, "that you think he might have followed her to town and then killed Sir James in jealousy?"

"Possibly," I said. "That would certainly be one motive if he thought the young woman's employer had supplanted him in her affections. But there could also be the motive of robbery if the young man again tried to steal. Or perhaps, if he was hiding from the police, he was afraid that Sir James would have him arrested."

The train slowed as we came to our station, and Sam Shakespeare, his pipe now gone out, seemed to breathe a sigh of relief. "I knew I was doing the right thing," he said, "when

I went to see you and Lord Tigraines in London. If only you had still been at Longmoor, the case might already be solved."

Waiting for us on the platform was Fred Quint, his eyes shining just as they had on the day Susan first went away. "Oh, Mr. Howard," he said, as I stepped off the train, "you must help my daughter. You must. She is a good girl. She was always an angel. The only wrong she ever did was to leave."

"Yes, Fred," I said to him, "I remember. I am here to do what I can."

Six

*I*t was true that I remembered Susan then in a way that I had not before. When I had first gone to work for his lordship, our visits to the estate had been rare. We were as likely to be in Florence, the Alps, the villa in France, or Madrid. But on those occasions when we did go to Longmoor, all the servants who had their own children, or even a nephew or niece, would dress them up and have them wait in the hall to curtsy and bow to their lord.

Lord Tigraines, I thought at first, disliked children; but in this I found I was wrong. One day one of the little girls had a bouquet of flowers for him, and those flowers, colorful in a place that had been gloomy since the death of his wife, seemed to touch him as nothing else could. Reaching down, he took the girl by the hand and led her to her ladyship's portrait where he had the flowers put in a vase.

"She is the daughter of the gardener," he said to me later, "and those flowers were just the kind my wife liked. It is a pity the little girl has no mother, nor even a good dress to wear."

That Christmas she did get a good dress, though his lordship, misjudging her size, had it made too large for her. She was a pretty child who grew awkward and shy. In her father's cottage she would stay in her room when his lordship and I went to call, and the only times we ever met on the grounds were when she was on her way back from school. On that day when we went to town to the play, she was the last of the group whom I would have thought likely to run away, just as now it was hard to believe that of all the people in Marley she was the one who was accused of this crime.

"Have you seen her yet?" I asked Fred Quint, as he drove us to the constable's office.

"I went to the jail twice," her father answered. "The first time Mr. Shakespeare came with me, but she would not refer to what happened. Mr. Ravenwood did not want her to talk."

"Not even to her father?" I asked.

Old Fred sadly shook his head. "I hope she is different with you, Mr. Howard," he said. "She always liked you, and she liked his lordship, too. Once she even kept a scrapbook, and in that scrapbook she put everything that had anything to do with the lord."

"From newspapers?" I asked.

"Yes," said Fred, "the illustrated ones. Sometimes the maids up at the house would give her one of those picture newspapers that showed his lordship with a lady in jewels. And she put them in the book."

"I am sure his lordship would be pleased to hear that," I said.

"But you must not tell him," said Fred. "My daughter would never want him to know. It was a secret that I only discovered when I found her with the scrapbook one day."

The small crowd that had been outside the bookstore when Sir James had first moved into town was insignificant compared to what we found now. Cars were parked on both sides of the street. Strangers who had the look of the cities were clustered outside the Green Fox, and at the jail, where Ravenwood had his office, a photographer had his camera set up. There had been something prophetic, I thought, in what Sir James had said when we first met. However celebrated he might have been in his life, he had become far more famous in death. Again, as so often before, crime outweighed other achievements. The murder meant more than the man.

"Well," Tom Ravenwood said to me when I arrived at his office, "I suppose that you and Lord Tigraines have come back to solve the mystery."

"Not his lordship. He is still in London," I said.

The constable smiled, appearing to take satisfaction from what, at least in the beginning, Sam Shakespeare had found disappointing. "So he has sent you alone then," he said. "That must mean his lordship has some faith that I will not completely bungle things."

"Lord Tigraines never thinks in those terms," I told him. "His concern, as it always has been, will merely be to see that justice is done."

"And what of the fact," the constable asked, "that a suspect in the case is the daughter of his lordship's gardener? Will that in any way influence him?"

"His lordship will consider that," I said. "But I am not sure, from his point of view, that she is a suspect at all. Would you mind telling me what sort of evidence you have been able to uncover so far?"

"Certainly I will tell you," he said. "I will tell you and the whole world at once when the inquest is held tomorrow. I may be a local constable, and not thought much of in the press or in the circles in which Lord Tigraines moves; but I also want to see justice done. I will not make the innocent suffer, nor do I think, since I have made one arrest, that the entire case has been solved."

"Then," I said, "you must believe that the girl is innocent, too."

"You will have to wait for the inquest to learn that," he answered. "My whole case, everything that I know, will be laid bare for all to see then."

The constable took me up to the jail, but I learned no more from the girl than her father and Sam had earlier. It even seemed that instead of a reassurance, my presence was troubling to her. "Does his lordship know about this?" she asked.

"He knows, and he will help you," I said.

She turned away. "That is awful," she said. "That is the worst thing of all."

Susan had changed. She was no longer the child with the flowers and the books on her arm. Her face, though it still appeared young, had the lines of experience now. Could it have been true, I wondered, that this was not her first time in jail? Could she have taken part in a robbery and in a young thief's escape? Looking at her through the bars of the cell, I realized somewhat to my surprise that she had actually become beautiful.

"What do you think?" asked Sam Shakespeare when I met him, as we had arranged, at a table in the Green Fox.

"I think his lordship should be here," I said. "Susan is innocent. I do not doubt that. But I do not like having her kept in jail."

I explained to him what Ravenwood had told me, and that the inquest would be held the next day. But then I also described Susan's face as I had seen it looking out through the bars. "I really think she could be an actress," I told him. "She may be shy. She may need to be trained. But with those eyes and that expression of pain, she has the look of a tragic heroine."

"A Juliet, you must be thinking," Sam said.

"Yes," I said, "or even a Joan of Arc."

Sam shook his head. "Our job then," he said, "will be to save her from hanging so that she can be burned at the stake."

In spite of the crowd in the Green Fox, and the reason so many were there, all the talk at the other tables appeared at first to be of cricket matches, a race, and which streams were best for fishing. But gradually everyone became quiet. All ears seemed to be listening to us, as Sam and I, in hushed tones, were trying not to let anyone hear.

When we left, a man with a notebook followed us all the way to the car where Fred sat patiently at the wheel. We got inside, and as Fred started off, the man began taking notes. What he had noticed, I thought, was his lordship's coat of arms on the door.

Seven

*I*nquests in the town of Marley were usually informal affairs. I had attended one when a previous owner of Redland had fallen and struck his head on a rock. That case, sensational as it was, had drawn so few spectators, though, that when we traveled out to the estate in order to examine the rock, we did not even crowd the sidewalks. The usual site of inquests, as well as of other civic events, was the little building called the Chamber of Marley, which in the days before Henry VIII had been the chapel of a nunnery. The chamber was too small for the present hearing, however. When I arrived, expecting it to be there, a sign directed me to Whitcross Hall, a far larger and more imposing structure located in the neighboring town.

Dr. Simpson, who himself lived in Whitcross, was testifying when I entered the room. He had examined the body, he said, and except for a bruise on the head and marks of trauma on the upper left arm, there were no signs of physical violence or that the deceased had done anything more than collapse and fall down on the stairs as a result of what the doctor termed "the ingestive insult of poison."

The coroner, a former military officer, was sensitive to any disturbance and banged his gavel at that point. Since it was a warm day and the air was close in the room, it was hard to tell if there was actual whispering or only a flutter of fans. But whatever it was, it was soon silenced, and the doctor was able to proceed.

The victim's face, Dr. Simpson continued, had what he called the look of the plague, which had led him to perform tests for arsenic. Both the Reinsch and Marsh tests were performed on the contents of the victim's stomach, and the presence of arsenic was confirmed. Furthermore, it appeared to be present in an unusual quantity. Though the time of death could not be determined with any great accuracy, the doctor said that most likely it had been between two and four hours before midnight.

"Are you able to tell us," the coroner inquired, "how this poison was consumed?"

"The victim had been drinking wine," said the doctor. "There was no sign that this was a habit. His liver and other organs were in a state of remarkable health. But that night he did a great deal of drinking."

"If it was not a habit," the coroner asked, "were you able to determine any reason that Sir James drank so much on that night?"

"The poison itself," said the doctor. "One of the effects of arsenic is to cause the victim to develop a thirst."

"I see," the coroner said. "Thank you, doctor. I am sure the implications of that are evident to everyone here. You may step down, and I will call the next witness."

The next witness was Constable Ravenwood and as the constable got up from his chair, I noticed that the person beside him was Susan Quint. She was dressed in a modest gray coat and veiled hat that I had seen worn by the constable's wife. Had she not turned when the man beside her got up, I would have thought it was Mrs. Ravenwood there. But Mrs. Ravenwood did not have such a chin, molded as if by a sculptor, nor did Mrs. Ravenwood have such eyes, luminous even under the veil.

The constable, after ascending the steps to what was almost a theater stage, raised his hand and was sworn in. Then the coroner began questioning him: "Would you tell us first, Constable Ravenwood, how you came to learn of the death, and who it was that reported it to you?"

"It was reported to me by a young woman," said the constable. "She was in the employ of the deceased."

"Was she a servant?" asked the coroner.

"That is correct," said the constable, "but she did not live at the house. She would arrive every morning at seven in order to serve Sir James his breakfast."

"What is this servant's name?" the coroner asked.

"Her name is Susan Quint," said the constable, "but she calls herself Quintleigh now."

"Is there a reason," the coroner asked, "for this change in the young woman's name?"

"She has aspired to be an actress," said the constable.

"Then when she testifies," the coroner said, "I trust she will have an actress' voice, so that all our spectators can hear. Would you please continue, Constable Ravenwood, and inform us of what this young woman told you and of what you learned yourself after that?"

Constable Ravenwood, who was in uniform, seemed uncomfortable before the large audience. While he spoke, he looked down at his feet, which he would shift back and forth as if his shoes were a little too small. "Well," he said, "this young woman—I will call her Miss Quintleigh—came to me at eight o'clock in the morning and was in an agitated condition. Her first words were, 'Please, you have to come,' and it was only after she was calmed by my wife that I was able to learn from her what had happened. She had arrived at her place of employment at approximately seven o'clock. This was the first time she had been there in three days since she had not been feeling well, and naturally she found things in confusion."

"What do you mean by confusion?" asked the coroner.

"I mean," said the constable, "that during her absence there had been no one to do the dishes, or to take care of other things in the house."

"I see," said the coroner. "Please proceed, constable."

"She cleaned the pans," the constable said, "and started cooking breakfast. But then she noticed something unusual. Normally, as soon as she arrived, she would hear Sir James moving about in the house. This morning she heard no such sounds, and so she stopped for a moment to listen. That was when she heard the whimpering."

"Did you say whimpering?" the coroner asked.

"That is the way Miss Quintleigh described it," said the constable. "She left the kitchen and went into the hall, where she saw sir James' dogs on the stairs. The two dogs were standing guard by their master and were the ones that had been making the noise. Even from a distance Miss Quintleigh could see that Sir James was in the posture of death."

"Then what did she do?" asked the coroner.

"She came to me," the constable said, "and I returned with her to the house where we found the dogs roaming the yard. They had set up such a barking and howl that the Shakespeares from next door came over. Sam—I mean Mr. Shakespeare—tried to help in pacifying the dogs, but they were far too ferocious for us. It was Susan—Miss Quintleigh, I mean—who finally led them back to the house where she locked them up in the cellar."

"Did the dogs obey her without difficulty?" asked the coroner.

"No," said the constable, "not without difficulty, but Miss Quintleigh was really quite fearless. When she took one of them by the collar, I thought it was going to bit off her hand."

Sam Shakespeare, in the front row, was nodding, and there

was a murmur of awe in the room. "All right, constable," the coroner said, "please go on. Tell us what you found in the house."

"What I found was that Sir James was dead," said the constable, "as Dr. Simpson has described him to you. Naturally, my assumption at first was that he had died of a heart attack. Not until Dr. Simpson arrived did we discover that Sir James had been poisoned."

"Did you discover the poison?" asked the coroner.

"No," said the constable, "I did not."

"No poison at all?" the coroner asked. "Not even a rodenticide?"

"A rodenticide?" asked the constable.

"A poison for rodents," the coroner explained. "Something to kill mice and rats with."

"In the basement I found a mousetrap," said the constable.

"But mousetraps do not use poison," said the coroner. "As a lure for mice, they use cheese."

"Yes," said the constable.

"Then did you find nothing else?" asked the coroner. "Was there no box with a skull and crossbones on it or no bottle that was labeled arsenic?"

"No," said the constable, "there was not."

"And I suppose," the coroner said, "that you have searched thoroughly."

"Very thoroughly," said the constable.

"Then did you discover," the coroner asked, "the means for administering the poison? You have said the dishes had not been washed."

"Not all of them," the constable answered, "but I told you Miss Quintleigh had started washing up."

"You told us she started with the pans," said the coroner.

"She started with the pans," said the constable, "but then she went on to the dishes. There were plates, cups and saucers, and glasses. When Dr. Simpson arrived, we looked at them, but it was too late to find poison then."

"Was there a bottle?" the coroner asked. "If the man had been drinking, there must have been a bottle."

"There was a wine bottle, yes," said the constable. "It was empty and had been left on the kitchen table. Unfortunately, though, for reasons she can explain, Miss Quintleigh had been washing it, too. She had put it in to soak with the dishes."

Eight

The effect of the constable's statement was to render even the coroner speechless, while the reporters and spectators gasped. Standing up in the rear, I turned at once to look at Susan whose head was lowered as she sat in her chair. From a distance, as the coroner banged the gavel, she had the look of someone bowing in prayer.

"Do you mean to say," the coroner said at last, "that this young woman has destroyed evidence? Has she removed every trace of the crime?"

"Not completely," the constable answered. "We do still, of course, have the body, and we have evidence of someone else in the house. Sir James, I think we can be certain, was not alone on the night of the crime."

"Then please go on," the coroner told him. "Let us hear who this other person was."

"His name is Staughton," the constable said, "but like Miss Quintleigh, he prefers to be known as something else. Rather than Timothy Staughton, he calls himself Timothy Loft."

"Is he someone with the same aspirations?" asked the coroner.

"That is right," the constable said. "He has also been on the stage. Both Mr. Loft and Miss Quintleigh performed in the same acting troupe that set up its tent here at Marley. Appropriately, they called themselves the Tent Players and specialized in comedy. Some may remember that when they were here they put on *She Stoops to Conquer*."

"I remember that myself," said the coroner, "and it was a play I thought they did very well. The vicar was sitting right behind me, and I heard him whisper in the middle of the performance that he wished the author, Dr. Goldsmith, were there."

"Unfortunately," the constable said, "not everyone was of the same opinion. The troupe developed a bad reputation, and many towns would not let them appear. This was not only because of their plays, but because of certain other matters which there is no need to go into here."

"And why is that?" the coroner asked. "I am sure our jury would like to hear anything that pertains in any way to the case."

"But these matters do not pertain to the case," said the constable, "and I would prefer to leave them out altogether. I am sorry I mentioned the troupe's reputation, since the only thing of importance is that although it could still draw a crowd, it was soon faced with debt and bankruptcy. Even worse, when Mr. Loft left the troupe, the cashbox of receipts was to go with him. He was tracked down and arrested in York, where he was found in the company of Miss Quintleigh. The court there was about to go into session, but before he could be put on trial, he escaped and has not been seen since. I had already had inquiries about him when Miss Quintleigh first came back to town, but I held back from taking action with her on the chance that Mr. Loft might come, too."

"In other words," the coroner interjected, "you were using Miss Quintleigh as bait in order to catch the villain."

"Not entirely," the constable said. "I am a friend of the Shakespeares, as you know, and the Shakespeares both swear by Miss Quintleigh. Also her father is the gardener Fred Quint, who works for his lordship at Longmoor. In view of both of these circumstances, I hesitate to say I used Miss Quintleigh as bait. But I did think her presence in Marley might lead to the arrival of the young man."

"And did it, Constable Ravenwood?" asked the coroner.

"That is what the evidence indicates," the constable said. "When I say Sir James was not alone in the house, it is because someone was living with him. Not Miss Quintleigh. She lived in town, and she may well be as innocent of this crime as she was of any other before. The person to whom I now refer occupied the servants' quarters in back. His hair, judging by strands in the room, was of a light sandy color, and he was approximately six feet tall."

"We understand about the hair," said the coroner, "but I think the jury might be interested to know how you were able to determine his height."

"His height," the constable answered, "could be measured by the very clear imprint left on the mattress of the bed. Also a pair of trousers and a shirt, which were found in a closet, had been made to fit someone that size. Needless to say, the height and hair color match those of Timothy Loft, and I am as sure he was the one in that room as I would be if he had left a picture behind."

"What does Miss Quintleigh have to say about it?" asked the coroner.

"That," said the constable, "is something you will have to ask her yourself. So far, in my interrogations, she has talked quite freely of herself, but she will neither confirm nor deny that her friend was ever there in the house."

"In that event," said the coroner, "Miss Quintleigh will be our next witness. Constable, I have no further questions. Unless you have something you wish to add, please step down."

The constable, as his testimony was ending, had ceased to shift his feet back and forth and was able to face the room of spectators with a look of professional pride. "I have only one last statement," he said, "and that is that people may be assured that this killer will not go unpunished. I have already sent a message to London to request the help of Scotland Yard, and an inspector should be arriving here shortly. The resources of his organization, added to my own knowledge of the case, should bring this investigation to a speedy and successful conclusion."

"You are to be commended," to coroner said. "Please step down."

Nine

The young Susan, before she mounted the steps, had removed the hat with the veil. But in spite of the warmth of the room, she still wore Mrs. Ravenwood's coat. The way it hung loose at her shoulders, with its sleeves almost hiding her hands, gave her the appearance of an orphan who had wandered in from a storm. The coroner, with his military posture, had been stiff with the previous witnesses, but after Susan was sworn in, he bent forward and spoke in a voice that was almost apologetic.

"Now, Miss Quintleigh," he began, "I know this case has been distressful for you; but since we hear you have been an actress, I hope you will respond to my questions as a character would in a play. Please do not think, if I seem to be prying, that my intention is either to embarrass or to entrap you into admissions of guilt. I am sure there is an innocent explanation for any involvement you yourself may have had."

Susan said nothing, but merely reached in a pocket for a handkerchief with which to wipe her nose.

"Please tell us first," the coroner continued, "how you came to work for Sir James and the kind of employer he was."

"It was the Shakespeares who sent me to him," Susan answered in a voice that could hardly be heard. "I was grateful to be given the work."

"Was your employer good to you?" the coroner asked.

"Sometimes he was," Susan said.

The coroner paused while Susan again wiped her nose. "You seem hesitant about that," he said. "I realize you may be reluctant to speak ill of someone who is dead, but nevertheless these questions are important. So far we have had no testimony on the character of the victim himself. His reputation, of course, is well known. He was a scholar and an important man in his field. But how was he in his personal life? Did Sir James go to church?"

"No," said Susan, "he did not go to church. Sir James had a different kind of religion. I am not exactly sure what you would call it, but he believed in reincarnation."

"In life after death?" the coroner asked.

"Yes," said Susan, "he asked what I thought of it once, and I told him that I did not know."

"Did Sir James often talk to you about death?" asked the coroner.

"Only once," Susan said. "Just when he asked that question."

"Then," said the coroner, "you do not believe that he was brooding over his own demise."

"Do you mean about suicide?" Susan asked.

"In a case of poisoning," the coroner explained, "suicide must always be considered. Was Sir James, in your opinion, the sort of man who might have taken his own life?"

"I would never have thought so," Susan said.

"Would you have thought," asked the coroner, "that he was the sort of person someone else might have wanted to kill? In other words, in his conversations with you, did he ever speak of enemies?"

"Not of enemies exactly," Susan said.

"Then of what?" asked the coroner.

"He did tell me once," Susan said, "that he had been unhappy as a child. He and his brother did not get along."

"Was there some reason he told you that?" asked the coroner. "Was he discussing this brother with you?"

"Yes," said Susan, "he was explaining to me the reason he never had married. He told me he had once thought of marriage, but the woman chose his brother instead."

"Did he ever speak of something more recent?" asked the coroner. "Did he ever mention his difficulties abroad, the kidnappings and other events that the newspapers tell us about?"

"No," Susan said.

"Then so far as you know," said the coroner, "there was no one who might have wished to kill him. Is that your answer?"

"Yes," Susan said, "that is my answer."

"We will move on then," the coroner said, "to what occurred on the morning Sir James was found dead. We understand from the constable's testimony that this was your first trip to the house in some time. May I assume, from the handkerchief in your hand, that the illness you suffered from was a cold?"

"Yes," said Susan.

"If you heard the constable's testimony," said the coroner, "is there something you want to add or subtract? Do you take exception to anything that he said?"

"No," said Susan.

"Then Constable Ravenwood was correct," said the coroner, "that when you arrived at the house you immediately started washing the dishes. Did you do this because it was your job, or did you have some other reason that day?"

"It was my job," Susan said.

"Was it a part of your job," asked the coroner, "to wash the wine bottle, too? I believe I can speak for the jury, and probably for everyone in this room, when I say this seems to be an unusual act."

"Yes, it was," Susan said. "The reason I put it in the water to soak was so that I could take off the label."

"And why," the coroner asked, "would you have wanted to do that?"

"So that I could use the bottle," Susan said. "I wanted to make it into a vase."

"A vase?" the coroner asked.

"For the kitchen window," Susan said. "It was green, and I thought it would look nice when it had the sun shining through it."

The spectators, who for a time had been still, were at last able to breathe again. It was as if the hall itself uttered a sigh, and when I looked at the faces of the jurors, the smiles were outnumbering the frowns. The coroner himself, however, seemed unhappy at Susan's explanation. His chivalry, it now appeared, had been nothing more than a pose, designed to catch her off guard. "Let me put this more directly," he said, once again with the tone he might have used in a military court. "Are you saying you had no intention of destroying evidence of the crime?"

"No," Susan answered.

"And what of this young man?" asked the coroner. "We know, from what the constable told us, that he was living in the house. Did you not think, when you found Sir James dead, that the young man had killed him?"

"No," said Susan, her voice growing stronger.

"But you do not deny," said the coroner, "that this fugitive from justice was there."

"He was not a fugitive from justice," Susan said. "He was a fugitive from injustice. Sir James understood that and helped him."

"And then this fugitive from injustice," said the coroner, "did the greatest injustice of all. He repaid Sir James by killing him.... You may step down now, Miss Quintleigh. We cannot excuse your dissembling, but the jury, when it deliberates, will undoubtedly take account of the fact that you are a young and impressionable woman whom it was easy for this robber to deceive."

Susan, instead of stepping down, walked to the middle of the platform, where she turned to face the whole room. "He was not a robber," she said, her voice firm enough for a Portia or even an Antigone. "If Timothy had stolen the cashbox, why would we have been so poor? We had to go from house to house to get food and for a roof over our heads. It may be true that we were fleeing accusers, but we were beggars, not thieves."

Ten

I would be exaggerating if I said that everyone in the room burst into applause. I applauded, as did Sam Shakespeare, as well as several others at first. But the coroner, banging his gavel, hammered us into silence. "The court is outraged," he shouted. "This witness has been asked to step down, but instead she keeps on talking. She answers when no question is asked her. She speaks when she is not spoken to."

Susan did step down after that, and other witnesses, including Sam Shakespeare, followed with their testimony. But for the most part they had little to add. The only really new information came from a Miss Jennifer Partridge, who on the morning when Sir James was found dead had been out on a back-country road, where she was observing the arrival of the first Marley wrens, identifiable by a crossbar on the back and an odd twist to the beak. Miss Partridge had heard the dogs bark, and then she had seen a young man with light hair running from the direction of Redland. She herself was at that time behind trees, so that she did not think she had been seen; but she had gotten a very good look at him.

"What did he look like?" asked the coroner. "Was there anything in the way he appeared that made you think he had committed an act such as the one that concerns us here?"

The lady, who was of a good Marley family, stood before us with great dignity. Until then she had spoken with all the poise that one might have expected from the president of the local chapter of the Society of Passerines. But now Miss Partridge appeared flustered. "The young man was running," she said.

"Was that all?" the coroner asked. "What about his face? Please describe it to us."

"I am afraid," said Miss Partridge, "that I cannot describe his face as you appear to want me to. There was nothing in the young man's face that made me think he was a criminal."

"Then what did you think?" asked the coroner.

"He had the face of an Adonis," she said.

The coroner had certainly done his best to solve the case through his sharp questioning, but in the end he was forced to give up. In his instructions to the jury, he said the only thing to be done was to leave matters in an unresolved state, which was something the jury then did. Those good people, who were shopkeepers, farmers, and a teacher who had known Susan in school, adjourned without reaching a verdict. No case had been proven, they said; and though Sir James, in his death by poison, might well have been the victim of murder, they believed the best course to follow was to await future investigations by the constable and Scotland Yard.

Since Susan would no longer be kept in jail, there was some doubt at first as to whether she should go back to the furnished room where she had lived in the town or to her father's cottage at Longmoor. I told her that if she had any thought that her father did not want her back, she was completely mistaken. "Your father loves you and always has," I said. "The only reason he did not come to the inquest was that he thought you would not want him to."

"I know," said Susan. "If I could please go back to town, I will return Mrs. Ravenwood's hat and coat, and then pack up the things in my room."

When a man is single as I always have been, the behavior of the other half of our species may strike him as more wonderful and strange than it would someone who is married and encounters it everyday. Of course, even a man like myself does have some friendship with women, but it is rare that he will feel the closeness that I felt with Susan on that drive. We spoke little, and there seemed no need to speak. When we stopped at the constable's house, she got out of the car and ran up to the door without my having to tell her she should hurry. She also hurried in the packing in her room, which was in the home of an elderly widow whose own children had long since gone away.

"She is a good girl, Mr. Howard," said her landlady as we waited for Susan downstairs. "How could anyone ever have thought that she had poisoned that man?"

"People are fools, Mrs. Norcliff," I told her.

"Yes," she said, "and the biggest fool of all has to be that Constable Ravenwood. He even came here to make sure that Susan really had been sick. I told him I was the one myself who kept her from going to work. She was here in this house for three days, until the morning when she was not really well, but insisted that she should go back."

"Then there is no question," I said, "that she was here the night before."

"Absolutely none, Mr. Howard," said the widow. "Naturally, I go to bed early, but if she had gone out in the night, I would have heard her on the stairs."

We heard Susan on the stairs at that moment, as she came down with a battered valise that had been tied together with string. She was not smiling, but had a calm, happy look, like that of someone who had been lost and was found. She kissed the woman with whom she had been living, and the woman reached up and touched Susan's hair. "Remember what I told you now," said the widow. "Put all those foolish dreams out of your mind. Settle down and find a young man who loves you. He will help you forget all of this."

"Yes, Mrs. Norcliff," Susan answered. "I am going back to my father again."

"And your father is a good man," said Mrs. Norcliff. "We all respect Mr. Quint in this town. There is no one with a garden who does not wish for his touch, to make the flowers bloom as they do at Longmoor. Old Adam was a gardener, remember; and he was the first of God's sons. He made the flowers blossom in Eden."

We went outside, and I put the valise in the car, while the widow, who stood at her door, waved a final farewell to the girl. On the drive through town there were others who were waving, even Tom Ravenwood who was standing outside the jail. Everyone on the streets of Marley seemed glad that Susan was free and able to begin life again.

"You and the constable certainly had us worried," I told her. "When you refused to tell anyone what had happened, we did not know what to think."

"Mr. Ravenwood told me not to talk," Susan said. "He thought whatever I said might be bad if the real killer heard it. You see, I did destroy evidence when I put all those things in the sink."

"Yes," I said, "but the explanation you gave was a perfectly logical one. A wine bottle does make a good vase."

"I was going to fill it with daisies," said Susan, "and with willows and forget-me-nots."

"Of course," I said. "You are the daughter of your father. Are you going to take Mrs. Norcliff's advice and go back to being Susan Quint, or are you still going to use your new name?"

"What do you think I should do?" she asked.

"I think it would please your father," I told her, "if you went back to his name. When you marry, you will get a new one."

"Yes, when I marry," she said.

We turned in at the Longmoor driveway where her father was working by the gate. I had never thought of old Fred as an Adam, but that was certainly what he was. Waiting there for our return, he was pulling weeds, and among them were willows, as well as daisies and forget-me-nots.

Eleven

With Susan no longer in jail, my own involvement in the case had lost its former urgency. This is how I described the situation in a letter that I wrote to Lord Tigraines in London:

> Dear Lord Alfred,
> As you have probably learned from the press, the young lady about whom we were concerned has now been released from the jail; and if there ever was a finger of suspicion pointed in her innocent direction, such is no longer the case. It appears that Ravenwood held her in jail only for her own protection and to prevent her talking to reporters. She is back at Longmoor with her father, and it was my pleasure only this morning to meet her coming in from the fields, where she had gone for a walk. You would be surprised, I believe, at how beautiful she has become, and how her spirits still remain high in spite of everything that has happened.
> My own theory, which I discussed with Sam on the train, is that there might have been some involvement on the part of a young man whom Susan met in the acting troupe. He has had trouble with the police in the past, and now we find he was living at Redland at the very time Sir James was poisoned. The worst testimony against him comes from Miss Jennifer Par-

tridge, who observed him fleeing down a back road on the morning the man was found dead. Susan herself seems quite blind to the defects in her friend's character, but that is to her credit. One can always commend loyalty, even when it is misplaced.

The constable mentioned at the inquest that he has called on Scotland Yard for help in resolving the case, and an inspector named Anthony Bland has already arrived from London. He has not yet been out to Longmoor, but he has studied the scene of the crime and has been talking to people in town. According to Sam, whom he talked to at length, the inspector has an open mind and believes it possible that Sir James may even have committed suicide.

I will stay at Longmoor, of course, until I receive other instructions from you. Until then, gratefully as always, I remain at your service,

George Howard

Shortly after this letter was mailed, and before his lordship had a chance to reply, Inspector Bland, in the constable's company, did come to pay a visit to Longmoor.

The inspector looked much like his name. A man of medium height and build, he had the kind of anonymous face that is considered an asset in his profession. Only his eyes, which were constantly shifting, indicated that the face was a mask and that behind it worked the brain of a criminal investigator.

"This is Mr. Howard," the constable said, as I met the two men at the door. "Mr. Howard is his lordship's secretary and something of a detective in his own right."

"I am aware of that," said the inspector, his voice without regional accent or almost any inflection at all. "I saw a play about his lordship in London, and I noticed that it was the secretary who investigated most of the clues."

"That play was written more for laughter," I told him, "than as a record of what really took place. Lord Tigraines has his own methods when it comes to investigations. I always have to ask what he is thinking. He rarely asks questions of me."

"In that event," said the inspector, "you must be like Sir Bruce Nottingham, who is my superior at the Yard. He also has an inquiring mind, and always wants to know what is on mine."

"Sir Bruce is a friend of his lordship," I said, but the inspector did not seem interested. Already, as we passed through the hall, he had put his head into the room that was modeled after a salon at Ferney. Then moving on, he tapped at a suit of armor that was standing guard at the next door.

"This is the kind of thing I wished I had once," he said. "On those nights when I was out on patrol, a suit of armor would have saved many bruises."

"I think you would have found it hard to walk in," I told him.

"And even harder to run in," he said. "Yes, the criminals would have gotten away. What is this room?"

"It is the main drawing room," I said. "In the beginning it was the heart of the castle, after the Romans were driven away."

"Then it goes back a long way," said the inspector. "I have always liked these old houses. Do you think I could be given a tour?"

"Of course," I said. "Where would you like to start?"

Inspector Bland looked about. "I would like to go up those stairs," he said. "It seems to me we have seen enough here, and what I would like you to show me are the living quarters above."

We started up the stairs, but he stopped, pausing before her ladyship's portrait. "Who is that?" he asked.

"That is Lady Sasha," I told him. "Lady Sasha was Lord Tigraines' wife."

"She looks foreign," said the inspector.

"Her ladyship was Russian," I said. "In Russia she was a princess."

"Then," said Inspector Bland, "it must have been one of those arranged marriages."

"Oh, no, it was a love match," I told him. "They met at Yasnaya Polyana, which was Count Leo Tolstoy's estate. Lady Sasha was a relative of Count Tolstoy."

"And had a striking face," said the inspector.

We proceeded up to the second floor, where the inspector, without asking permission, kept trying doors to see where they led. "So many closets," he told me, as I showed him into my own room. "It is good no crime was committed here, since it would take the whole Yard to search it." He looked out the window. "And who is that there?" he said.

"Where?" I asked.

"There in the distance," he said. "A young woman is out in the fields."

"Oh, that is Susan Quint," I told him. "She is the one the constable first arrested, but now she has been completely cleared. She likes to walk around the estate."

"No harm in that," said the inspector. "No, I see no harm there at all. Well, Mr. Howard, if we could sit down and talk, I think I have seen enough of the house."

As we went back down the stairs, the inspector paused again at the portrait. "Yes," he said, "she had a most striking face. That must be why his lordship never remarried, even though it means he has no heir."

"His lordship's heir is his younger sister," I told him. "She lives in Ireland with her husband, and we rarely see them at Longmoor now. She is married to Sir Michael McNaught."

"Captain McNaught," said the inspector. "I remember him as the hero of Kimberley. He was wounded there, though, was he not?"

"He lost an arm," I said.

"Yes," said the inspector, "just like Lord Nelson. He is a fine man, from everything I have heard."

I took the constable and the inspector into his lordship's library, and there the three of us sat on chairs that at times had been occupied by some of England's and the world's greatest men. There had even been an occasional woman who had graced the room with her superior presence.

"This is a very impressive room," said the inspector, his eyes moving from the busts of the ancients to a photograph behind my head. "By any chance, is that H. Rider Haggard? I have read his books ever since my boyhood."

"Yes, that is Sir Henry," I told him. "But his interests now are in farming and in doing what he can for the poor. As you must know, he is on a Royal Commission, traveling all over the world."

"That only takes him from his writing," said the inspector. "I always liked his Allan Quatermain. Do you suppose the man himself is like that?"

"Every inch and even more," I answered, "which is very unusual. Authors rarely resemble the people whom they write about, though Oscar Wilde was another exception. His lordship says that to meet him in person was to meet a character who belonged on the stage."

"Did Lord Tigraines know Oscar Wilde?" asked the inspector.

"They met in Cairo," I told him, "and afterwards remained friends to the end. Lord Tigraines was not like some others who deserted him after the trial."

"I have heard his lordship was steadfast," said the inspector, "and I only regret that in my profession it is sometimes necessary to place official duties above such personal loyalties. In a case like this one, which has brought me to Marley, I look about at the town and tell myself the people seem virtuous. I have met the solicitor, Mr. Shakespeare. I have met the vicar, Mr. Halliday. I have been to your shops, your post office, and another place you may know, the Green Fox. Everywhere I meet good English people, the kind of people who make sense of the fact that our Empire has been given dominion over so much of the earth. Then I learn this is also the home of one of the greatest peers of the realm. I find he has a secretary, a most pleasant man, who is actually from America. And I learn, too, that the lord has a gardener, whose daughter, an aspiring actress, worked in the house of a man who has been poisoned. I tell myself it seems wrong to suspect that one of these people—anyone in this town—could have perpetrated a murder. But unfortunately a murder has been committed, and someone must be at fault."

"Have you decided that it was a murder then?" I asked. "I was told by someone you talked to that you thought it might have been suicide."

"Then you have been talking to Mr. Shakespeare," he said. "I did discuss that possibility with him, and for a while I found myself leaning toward it. But certain facts, when carefully scrutinized, point in a different direction. First of all, no suicide note was found. That may not, by itself, be conclusive, since many who commit suicide leave no notes. But then again there are also not many who collapse as Sir James did on the stairs. I have found that if a man takes a poison he will usually do it in his bed or when sitting in a bath or a chair. In other words, he will compose himself and then await the effect stoically. Let us say, though, that he intends to do this, but at the last moment changes his mind. That might explain why he would fall on the stairs, but it would not explain other things in this case."

"I am afraid you have me at a disadvantage," I said. "I am not sure what you mean by other things."

"Other things," said the inspector, "that would be inconsistent with the idea that Sir James killed himself. Someone who commits suicide, I have generally found, will try to tidy things up when he goes. If he keeps accounts, he will put them in order. If he has a diary, he will fill in the last page. If he is writing a letter, he will complete it and at least sign his name."

"And Sir James did not do those things?" I asked. "I was not aware that he had a diary."

Inspector Bland, for the first time, allowed a smile to come to his lips. "Yes," he said, "I do see what you mean when you say you are the one who asks questions and his lordship answers them. Sir James both had a diary and was in the process of composing a letter. The diary itself is an old one. It is what I think you might call a workbook, filled with drawings of pottery and statues and the most meticulous notes on how each item was found. In addition, though, there are personal matters. There are several references to someone identified only as N. This N, at least on one occasion, appeared to Sir James in a dream."

"N could be Nimrod," I told him. "Sir James wrote a book about him."

"That thought has occurred to me, too," said the inspector. "But in any case, the diary is an old one, and it is the letter that is of most interest. This letter, which as I say was unfinished, was dated the very day of his death and appears intended for someone in town."

"No such letter was mentioned at the inquest," I said.

"Indeed not," responded the inspector. "Constable Ravenwood very wisely decided that since the letter was of an innocent nature, and on the surface did not deal with the crime, it had no place as evidence. But to you, when we discuss suicide, I can see this letter takes on importance. It establishes two basic facts. The first is that since the letter was unfinished, the victim must have intended to go back and complete it at some later time. And the second fact of interest to a detective is that the victim had a friend in the town. Though it may have been assumed by some people that Sir James was something of a recluse, he was not totally isolated. In addition to the girl, his housekeeper, and the young man living in the back room, there was someone else who took an interest in him."

"May I ask who that was?" I said.

"Certainly you may," said the inspector, "but I would rather ask you. Since you know the people here better than I do, whom do you think he might have been writing to?"

"I suppose it could have been anyone," I said. "His lordship had Sir James as a guest at our New Year's banquet this year. Sir James was impressive to people, and particularly, I think, to the ladies. Was the letter, by any chance, to a woman?"

"It could have been," said the inspector. "Suppose it was; which of the ladies in town would seem the most likely to you?"

"I have no idea at all," I told him. "I think, in fact, that I will have to give up and let you tell me the answer yourself."

Inspector Bland had given no indication that he was doing anything more than playing a kind of game with me. Now, though, a frown came to his brow. "All right," he said, "I will admit something to you. The letter does not mention a name."

"But how is that possible?" I asked.

"It merely says, 'My Dear Friend,' " said the inspector. "That is the salutation, and in what follows there is nothing to indicate whether this friend was a woman or a man."

"Were there other letters in the house?" I asked.

"That is a most excellent suggestion," said the inspector. "I see now why his lordship is so fortunate to have a man like yourself on his staff. Yes, a search has been made for such letters, but unfortunately none has been found."

"Then the letter, too, is a mystery," I said. "It will have to be searched for its clues."

"Perhaps you would like to read it yourself," said the inspector, as he drew a folded sheet from his pocket. He handed the sheet to me. When I unfolded it, I saw that there were only a few lines. This, to the best of my recollection, is what the letter contained:

My Dear Friend,

Since the last time we saw each other, I have given a great deal of thought to some of the things that you said. Our paths are different, and it does not seem wise, from either your point of view or my own, for us to struggle against the impossible.

Twelve

After reading the letter, I folded the sheet once again and handed it back to the inspector, who waited for me to speak.

"Yes, I do see your problem," I said. "It is hard to tell anything about that letter except that the two of them must have met and had some sort of discussion. The other person could have been a woman, if the impossible was the emotion of love, but it could also have been a man who was on a different path in some way."

"In either case they would have been on different paths," said the inspector, with what appeared to be impatience. "If the person written to was a woman, then that woman may well have been married. And if she was married, there would be a husband involved."

"Not just a husband, but a motive," I told him. "The husband may have felt jealousy."

"That could well be true," said the inspector, "but nevertheless there are still certain problems. We must identify the intended recipient, and then we must overcome the difficulty of the dogs. If you were present at the inquest, you must be aware that the constable and Mr. Shakespeare had a problem in controlling them."

"I had the same problem myself once," I told him. "When I went to invite Sir James to the banquet, the dogs would not let me out of the car."

"Then," said the inspector, "your experience was the same. Aside from Sir James himself, apparently only the girl Susan knew how to make them behave. Sir James, since he arrived here from France, must have acquired the dogs quite recently, and perhaps there was not enough time to train them in the meeting of strangers. Or else, and this may be more likely, Sir James did not welcome strangers himself."

"Lord Tigraines has often said," I commented, "that the behavior of a dog reflects the state of mind of its master."

"There is truth in that," the inspector agreed. "More than one seemingly harmless person has been unmasked by the bark of his dog. But in this particular case, of course, the dogs belonged to the victim. We must seek elsewhere for the savage who sent Sir James to his grave. Mr. Shakespeare has told me that you believed the young man to be guilty. Has something happened to change your mind about that?"

"Before I heard about the letter," I said, "he did seem to be the principal suspect."

"And not now?" asked the inspector.

"Not if it can be shown," I said, "that there was someone else with a motive. You must know that the Shakespeares heard shouting, which would mean, if the voices were real and not from a Gramophone, that Sir James was in company with a woman. I do not think I need to add that it could well be this same woman to whom he wrote on the day of his death."

"We will explore that," said the inspector, leaning forward in his chair. "I have heard about the shouting incident. Though Sir James did have a Gramophone, it is possible the voices were real. But if there was such a woman, Sir James must have parted with her. Why, after they had parted, would he write the kind of letter he did? And why, on the very day of writing this letter, was he to die of poisoning?"

"Because they saw each other in town," I suggested. "They had a rendezvous. When the woman's husband found out, he decided to poison Sir James."

"Very good," the inspector said, leaning back. "It begins almost to fit together. But now we come to the murder itself.

How did this husband have access to the house? How did he get past the dogs, and then how, by what devious means, was he able to administer the poison?"

"That we will learn when we find him," I said. "Once the connection is established, he will almost be forced to confess. After all, even at this very moment, the secret is not his alone. His wife must know what he has done, and in time she herself may come forward. If not, there could be a new murder when the husband decides to kill her."

Inspector Bland turned to the constable who had been silent through all this. "It seems," the inspector said to him, "that Mr. Howard does not share your view that no murderers live in this town. He is contemplating, in fact, a second murder in order to cover up the first."

"In that event," said the constable, "why not ask who this murderer is? That is the only thing of importance, and that is where not only Mr. Howard but Lord Tigraines himself will be stopped. It is easy to dream up these theories, but a theory does not make an arrest."

The inspector turned back to me. "Well," he said, "what do you say to that?"

"All I can say," I answered, "is that Constable Ravenwood has a point. Theory is little good without fact, and the facts in this case are too few. Perhaps we have even made a mistake in assuming the letter Sir James was writing was intended for someone in town. It could just as easily have been to someone in London, to a rival scholar or a person like that."

"Yes," the inspector said, "so it could have. And you are raising an interesting point. Up to now the motive we have discussed has been the usual one of jealousy. But Sir James was a figure of controversy. Is it possible there were people in town who did not approve of him?"

"They bought his books," I said. "His books sold out at once."

"So the bookseller told me," said the inspector. "As a matter of fact, you yourself, I believe, were among the first to purchase one."

"I bought *The Descent of Ishtar* for his lordship," I said.

"Was Lord Tigraines an admirer of Sir James?" asked the inspector.

"His lordship," I said, "always has interest in anything to do with the ancient world."

"Then it must be true," said the inspector, as his eyes again surveyed the room, "that Lord Tigraines is a man of learning. But let me ask this final question. Do you know of anyone in the town who took a special dislike to Sir James because of the sort of things he had written? Did the vicar, for example, ever express his disapproval to you?"

"The vicar," I said, "would be the one whom you should ask about that. I know Mr. Halliday only as a man who delivers pious and entertaining sermons."

"Has Mr. Halliday," asked the inspector, "never been a visitor to this house?"

"Oh, yes," I said, "he was even here with Sir James on the occasion of the New Year's banquet. But they had no argument, if that is what you mean."

"I see," said the inspector, getting up. "I was asking only because the vicar showed reluctance in having Sir James buried on the church grounds. His reason was perfectly logical. He said he thought Sir James' relatives should decide on the last resting place. But nevertheless a policeman, as you know, must look behind outer motives, no matter how sensible they may seem."

"Yes, of course," I said, getting up, too. "Have you heard from Sir James' relatives?"

"So far no," said the inspector. "He has a brother, but we have not heard from him. The brother lives in South America, we believe, and may not know of the death."

I walked the two men to their car, and was relieved, after they drove away, that neither of them had asked to see Susan Quint, who had already been through enough.

Thirteen

*I*t was two days after this visit, and before I wrote to his lordship again, that I received the following communication from him:

> My Dear George,
> Your letter arrived, and I was most pleased to read, as it was also reported in the press, that our Susan was never under suspicion. I was sorry not to return to Longmoor with you, but as you know there were a number of engagements, not all of which could be postponed. Furthermore, my faith in your abilities, as well as in those of Sam Shakespeare, was sufficient to keep my mind at ease on the ultimate outcome of the case. Now that you say Inspector Anthony Bland has been called in from Scotland Yard, I am even more certain that all will turn out for the best.
> I have never met the inspector myself, but I have been assured by Sir Bruce Nottingham, who is his superior at the Yard, that he is a man of discernment and discretion. His past work has included the solution to the puzzling "Tapestry Case," in which the victim, held captive by her killer, was able to weave

an apple and a gate into the design on her loom. Inspector Bland, I have been told by Sir Bruce, was the one who interpreted this as referring to someone named Applegate, a cousin and heir then revealed as one of England's most heartless killers.

In recent days I have had several theories of my own on the possible murderer of Sir James, and I have even gone to some lengths in an attempt to establish the facts. Unfortunately I must suspend this, however, because of news that has just been received. My sister and her husband, who were out on a cruise, appear to have had difficulty. No one believes it could be serious, but I am leaving to join in the search. If I find I need you for some reason, I hope you will be prepared to come, too.

There were other things in the letter, but since they involved only household details, I will leave them out of this account. What was important was that his lordship had himself been doing work on the case (though what this was he did not say), and that his sister and brother-in-law, Lady Mary and Sir Michael McNaught, were apparently missing at sea.

Lady Mary I had met many times, and a finer woman could not be imagined. As a Tigraines she, of course, had an air that to some may have seemed forbidding, but I had never found her so myself. Not once had I ever known her to speak a single word of unkindness. Instead she was always compaigning on behalf of those less fortunate than herself.

She had been a nurse during the Boer War; and the story was told, though never by herself, of how, when an enemy soldier lay dying outside her camp, she went out in the night and rescued him. After the war, when she returned to England, she became a campaigner for peace, and she even gave a lecture in Marley on the importance of socialism. Lord Tigraines liked to say that his sister was the finest speaker he ever heard and could have been another Beatrice Webb if she had not married Sir Michael.

Sir Michael I did not know as well, but he was a quiet, even scholarly, person who, as an Irishman, had a soft, gentle brogue that made even the simplest of words sound as if they were poetry. He had met his wife during the war, when an arm had been blown from his side during the siege of Kimberley. It was thought he would die from loss of blood and infection, but he survived to come back to England, receive a knighthood, and marry his nurse.

Their wedding was remembered in Marley as one of the century's greatest events, and Lord Tigraines always respected Sir Michael. It was his lordship who had given Sir Michael the small yacht that he had learned to sail with one arm. When the daughter Ethel was born, one would have thought, from his feeling of pride, that Lord Tigraines himself was the father.

It gave me great apprehension to think that this couple, and perhaps the girl, too, might actually be lost to us now. Though I did not go to Ireland then to join Lord Tigraines in the search, there were reports every day in the papers, which did make it appear they had drowned. No longer was the death of Sir James the main topic of discussion in Marley. Whenever I went into the village, it was this new tragedy that was on everyone's lips.

There was still time, of course, for the gossip that Miss Partridge, before Sir James moved in, had liked to go to the Redland estate to watch a particular type of jay that nested in a broken chimney. Also I was to hear that the inspector had had three interviews with the vicar. But when I went to see the vicar myself, it was on the different matter of a prayer service for the McNaughts.

Fourteen

*T*he vicar received me in his study where, from the clutter of papers and open books stacked about, it seemed that he had been preparing a sermon. Someone once, in a wicked remark, had said that if Samuel Johnson was right, and a woman minister was like a dog on hind legs, the vicar was one on all fours. But if it was true that there was something doglike about him, this was mostly in the cheerful bark of his voice and in the friendly way, when congratulated on a sermon, that he would seem to be wagging his tail.

He was the conscience and comforter of a village whose people asked of him nothing more than that when they came to his church it should not be too much of a chore. One of the ways he kept their interest was with a humorous quotation or joke, but another was through the vision he offered of a world beyond what could be seen. Faith, he once said in a sermon, could lift a soul out of despair and into the pastures of beneficent love.

I had need of such faith now myself, and it seemed that the vicar may have, too. "I am certainly distressed," he told me, "when I hear that our brave Lady Mary has possibly been drowned at sea. Has Lord Tigraines sent no encouraging news?"

"Only about the daughter," I said. "Little Ethel was not with her parents. She was in the care of a housekeeper on shore."

"Thank goodness for that," said the vicar. "But are her parents now truly lost?"

"Lord Tigraines is still searching," I told him. "He says he has assembled a small navy to search every inch of the coast. So far, though, no wreckage has been found, and I know that I speak for his lordship when I say your offer of a prayer service is something greatly appreciated."

"It will be attended by the whole parish," said the vicar. "Many of us remember Lady Mary and the sweetness she had as a child."

Mrs. Halliday, who joined us for tea, expressed a similar sentiment. "I did not know Lady Mary as well as my husband did," she explained, "but people say she was a remarkable woman. You must have heard how she risked her life to save soldiers during the war."

"Yes," I said, "I have heard many stories. His lordship was always proud of her."

"They were almost like twins," said the vicar. "My wife does not remember those days because she did not live here then, but I myself came from a family in Whitcross. We were not in any way distinguished. My father was actually a poor man, who had a tanning and parchment business. But when I showed promise in school, I came to the attention of the old Lord Tigraines, the father of Lady Mary and Lord Alfred. His lordship may never have told you this, but my education was at the expense of his family. Even this parish, when it came to be offered, was given to me at the old lord's behest."

"You must have known the family well then," I said.

"Sometimes I flatter myself," said the vicar, "that I was a kind of adopted member. But Lord Alfred himself, naturally, was brought up in a different way. You may recall that with John Stuart Mill a special program was arranged so that Mill would become a scholar. I suppose the idea for that was something taken from Rousseau. His book Émile, though dedicated to nature, describes how a child should be raised; and with the examples of Mill and Rousseau, his lordship's father believed that his son could one day become prime minister. It is possible that it may still happen, but Lord Alfred learned a little too much."

"No one can learn too much," said Mrs. Halliday. "I admit there are very few subjects that his lordship is shy in discussing, but I would hardly call him a John Stuart Mill."

"He may be greater than Mill," said her husband. "Mill, after all, was a parrot who took his thoughts from his father, James Mill, and from his father's friend Jeremy Bentham. But his lordship, though he had some fine tutors, has gone on to be a student of life. There is a story, I think, of the Buddha, who was brought up in a similar way. The Buddha's father wished to make him a king, and for that purpose he had him kept in a garden where he would never see suffering and death. But the Buddha escaped from the garden, and outside he saw poverty, illness, and a corpse at the side of the road. The Buddha's kingdom became that of the spirit, since it is only the spirit that is able to transcend such things."

Mrs. Halliday put down her cup. "You must think it strange," she told me, "that my husband compares Lord Tigraines to the Buddha, or even speaks of the Buddha at all. But the vicar has been under a strain. I think it is time, George, you were told about what has been happening here and the way that man from Scotland Yard keeps coming to us with his suspicions."

"Now, my dear," said the vicar, "there is no cause to think me under suspicion. I have always performed my duties in the parish in the way that I considered best. I have been open and offered my counsel to anyone who seemed in need."

"But still George should be told," said his wife. "George has experience in these matters and can even get his lordship to help."

"Please, my dear," said the vicar, "George has come on a different matter. He is concerned about arrangements for the prayer service that I am having for Lady Mary and Sir Michael. The question of the death of Sir James, and my own possible involvement in it, must be the farthest thing from his mind."

"I would hardly say that," I said. "The prayer service was the reason I came, but if there is something about the death of Sir James that you feel involves you in some way, I would certainly like to hear about it."

The vicar took a sip of his tea. "It does not involve me," he said. "I am sure it does not. But I did have a relationship with Sir James that not many in the parish knew of. You may remember that when we were at the banquet I said something about his making a contribution to our understanding of the Biblical texts."

"I also remember," I told him, "that at the post office one morning you said something about the worship of idols. I believe you even called them obscene."

"Oh, yes," he said. "But that was only a joke. I am not at all the sort of narrow-minded man that such a statement might indicate. What I have told you about my own father was true. He was poor, but he was also an atheist. He and my anarchist grandfather were followers of that Frenchman Proudhon. 'God is evil.' That was one of their slogans."

"How," I asked, "could you have grown up in such a family and become a vicar yourself?"

"I was a flower in the desert," said the vicar. "But I was watered by the old Lord Tigraines. Through him I was to be the first, at least in these more recent times, who has attempted to restore holiness to the meaning of the Halliday name. I may have spoken harshly of Sir James. I may have called him an apostate at first, but his ideas were not unfamiliar."

"Did you see Sir James often?" I asked.

"Certainly not often," he said. "I did invite him to give a lecture at the church, but he did not want to do that. Where we met, actually, was in town, and then a few times on the road when he was taking an afternoon walk. We talked together and I felt we became friends. He did not try to push his ideas on me, and I did not push mine on him. We did agree, though, that religion is a far more ancient and sacred thing than most modern people believe."

"Did Sir James ever write to you?" I asked.

Mr. Halliday nodded. "That is what the inspector seems to think," he said. "A letter, begun but not finished, was discovered among his effects."

Fifteen

*I*t seemed unlikely that the vicar really could have been under suspicion. Instead, if he were the one to whom Sir James had been writing the letter, the letter itself would lose its significance, at least as a clue to the crime. I did my best to convince the vicar of this, and then returned to the car where I expected to find Susan Quint, who had come with me into town. When I found she was not there, however, I decided to stop in the bookstore, where I came upon Inspector Bland.

The inspector, who was browsing through a book on the history of bird-watching in England, appeared surprised to see me at first, but then quickly recovered himself. "This is a fortuitous meeting, Mr. Howard," he said, as he put the book back on its shelf. "Only yesterday I received a message from my superior, Sir Bruce Nottingham. As you may know yourself, Sir Bruce has been in touch with Lord Tigraines, and his lordship has made a number of suggestions toward the resolution of the case."

"His lordship mentioned something about that," I said, "but unfortunately he has been called away. He is now in Ireland."

"So I understand," said the inspector. "But his suggestions, even in his absence, are being pursued by the Yard. It seems that his lordship believes that the crime may somehow be connected with what happened to Sir James in the field. Twice he was held for ransom by brigands, and that is being investigated now. From the Yard's point of view, naturally, it hardly appears very likely that the brigands came all the way here and poisoned Sir James in the night; but any theory, in a case of this kind, merits some exploration. Lord Tigraines, as Sir Bruce has informed me, is also interested in the late Sir James' relatives, perhaps because, with royalties from the books, there may be a substantial estate."

"Have any relatives made a claim yet?" I asked.

"There have been no claims," said the inspector, "and the only relative of whom we have any knowledge is the brother who is in Paraguay. After the authorities there have responded to our inquiries, we may learn a good deal more about him. But in England there is no record of the brother since he left six years ago."

The inspector, I could not help noticing, kept shifting his eyes to the window. Through the window he could see up the street all the way to the door of the bank, where Constable Ravenwood was then standing. The constable reached to the brim of his hat, lifted the hat, and set it back again. That this was a signal there could be little doubt, for the inspector abruptly announced that he would have to depart. He left but did not head toward the bank. Instead he started in the opposite direction, and when I looked out the door, I saw him turn at the corner as if to circle the block.

The owner of the bookstore, Mr. Martree, seemed as puzzled by all this as I was. "Do you suppose the inspector has a suspect?" he asked. "He pretended to be interested in that book, but all the time he had his eyes on the window."

"Did the inspector say anything?" I asked.

"Not until you came," said Mr. Martree. "I did hear him telling you, though, about Sir James' brother in Paraguay, and I wanted to mention something about that. I suppose you know that the Jesuits at one time tried to run it as a utopia."

"No," I said, "I was not aware of that."

Mr. Martree, who was rarely disturbed in the tranquility of his shop, was as much a reader as a seller of books. People who bought books from him could see that, for he had the unfortunate habit of licking a finger whenever he turned a page, which would leave little smudges and marks. "Yes," he went on, "and then of course you remember that Candide and his friends went there, too. I wonder if Paraguay has jungles. It has mines, and so maybe this brother is one of those mining engineers."

"If he is," I said, "it probably means that he has no great financial problems. He would not kill his one relative merely for the inheritance."

Mr. Martree started to lick a finger, as if about to turn a page in his mind. "You are certainly right about that," he said. "And besides, I doubt very much that the royalties would make anyone rich. Perhaps now, since the man has been poisoned, there will be a flurry of sales. But such flurries never last very long. Sir James, though a respectable scholar and certainly a leading man in his field, always struck me as a very dull writer. His sentences are often longer than Gibbon's, but without the dazzle of that Erasmian mind. I consider the man's work important, but only in the sense that a footnote can be important to a page."

"Did you ever meet Sir James in person?" I asked.

"He came into the shop twice," said Mr. Martree. "The first time I asked if he would mind autographing the copies of his books that I was about to put on sale. It was a mistake on my part to have asked this, since Sir James called it commercialism. He told me I was trying to make profit from the fact that he had moved into town."

"Did he say anything else?" I asked.

"Yes," said Mr. Martree, "we talked for a while. I asked him what he thought of the theory that the goddesses Ishtar and Astarte had once been thought to be embodied in the meteorites found on the earth. Their names, after all, are quite close to the word *aster*, or star, and we know their great sister Cybele was worshiped in exactly that form. In order to drive off Hannibal, the sacred black stone of Cybele was placed on Rome's Palatine Hill."

"What did Sir James say to that?" I asked.

"Sir James told me," said Mr. Martree, "that speculations of that kind were of a literary character. He granted that sometimes literature can be of importance in understanding the past, but he claimed to base own work on more scientific techniques."

"He was an archaeologist to the core then," I said.

"Yes," Mr. Martree agreed, "and that may well be the reason that his work has such little value. It is a catalogue of minor discoveries dressed up in overblown prose."

"You tell me Sir James was here twice," I said. "Was this discussion continued the next time?"

"The next time we discussed gardening," said Mr. Martree. "Sir James, and he was perfectly right, said that his land had been going to seed. He wanted to see what other people did with estates such as his, and so I sold him a book called *The English Garden*. Since it has a section on Longmoor, you may be familiar with it."

"I most certainly am," I told him. "There is a picture of Fred Quint in it."

I left the shop and walked back to the car where I found that Fred's daughter was waiting. She seemed upset. When I asked what was wrong, she said that the most awful-looking man had been following her all over town. He had followed her to Mrs. Norcliff's, which was the place where she had been delayed. Then she saw him again on her way back. Once she thought he had even circled a block, in order to get behind her.

"I think I know who he was then," I said. "Was he that man who is across the street now, pretending to look in the window of the Green Fox?"

"Yes, Mr. Howard," she said, as Inspector Bland turned from the window and bowed in our direction. "How did you ever know that?"

Sixteen

*A*fter what had happened with Susan in town, I should not, perhaps, have been surprised when the constable's car, a buggy-like vehicle, came up the driveway the next day. This time, though, the constable and the inspector had brought with them the two dogs that had once belonged to Sir James. Constable Ravenwood, who was carrying a rifle, was the first to get out of the car. Then the inspector, while the constable kept his distance, pulled the dogs out after him.

"I am sure you know why we are here," said the inspector, as the dogs, straining against their ropes, stood on their hind legs to greet me.

"No," I said, looking from the dogs to the rifle that had an old shirt wrapped around it, "but I must tell you that if you have come for a hunt, it is forbidden on this land. Lord Tigraines is opposed to blood sports."

"We are not here for sport," said the inspector. "There has been a murder, and we have reason to believe that you are harboring a fugitive."

"What could possibly make you think that?" I asked.

"Merely the fact," the inspector answered, "that the fugitive, who was seen by Miss Partridge, has disappeared. No farmer has seen him in his fields. No traveler or keeper of an inn has reported seeing him on the road. Therefore, he must still be in Marley, and in Marley this is where he would hide."

"Do you have proof of that accusation?" I asked him.

"Not proof," the inspector admitted, "but an absence of proof, which in criminal investigations is called the process of elimination."

I was about to mention that I understood now why the inspector had followed Susan in town, but then I noticed that Susan and her father were approaching us along the hedged lane that led from their little cottage. Possibly they had heard the barking of the dogs, which Susan may even have recognized. But it was certain that when Susan saw the two men she recognized the inspector as the one who had been following her. Also she must have recognized the shirt that Constable Ravenwood had wrapped around the rifle, for I noticed that when she saw it her eyes widened with apprehension.

"This is Inspector Bland," I told the father and daughter. "He is the investigator from Scotland Yard whom we saw in town yesterday."

Susan said nothing, but approached the dogs, calming them with strokes behind their ears. The two dogs, it seemed, did like Susan, since at this sign of affection they both began wagging their tails.

"Has the inspector come for my daughter?" Fred asked.

"Not for your daughter," answered Inspector Bland, "but for the person your daughter is hiding. If she wishes to tell us where he is, no action will be taken against her. But if she does not, we are still going to find him, which will put her in jeopardy, too. Before the law, she will be an accomplice. When the fugitive goes on trial, a judge may very well want to rule that she has shared in his crimes."

"Timothy is innocent of any crimes," Susan said, her voice quavering with emotion very much like that of someone in love.

"He is at least a thief," said the inspector. "To that crime he has already confessed."

"No," she said, "you do not understand. If he ever took any blame on himself, it was only to protect me."

"And now you are protecting him," said the inspector. "That

is why we are going to search these grounds. Once the dogs begin sniffing the shirt that the young man left behind at Redland, they will lead us straight to him."

"Does that mean you are planning," I asked, "to turn those dogs loose on the grounds? Suppose they do find a traveler or vagrant living somewhere on the land. Lord Tigraines has always instructed that only kindness should be shown to such people. His lordship would want them to be fed and given whatever else they might need."

"Lord Tigraines is generous," said the inspector. "That is the kind of generosity, however, that often helps a fugitive to escape. We will be careful. I assure you of that. If all we find is a harmless vagrant, he will be turned over to you. Now, do you deny us permission so that a warrant will have to be obtained? Or will you yourself join in the search?"

"I will join you," I told him, "but only to prove you are wrong."

Searching Longmoor, I thought then, would not be as simple an undertaking as the inspector seemed to think. In addition to the grounds surrounding the house, there was a kind of wasteland beyond, with its hills, sunken caves, and the traces of ancient Romans. The inspector, taking the shirt from the rifle, waved it in front of the dogs. But they appeared confused by this and merely squatted back on their haunches.

"Are they hunting dogs?" I asked the inspector.

"All dogs are hunters," he said.

While the rest of us followed, the inspector led the dogs back to the gate and then along the path inside the wall where the inspector—not the dogs—discovered a place where a vine had been torn. "This is where he climbed over," said the inspector, "and there you see where he trampled that bush. He may have jumped or even fallen on it. Do you see that heel mark on the ground?"

Without doubt the inspector was right. Someone did seem to have jumped from the wall, or perhaps have fallen when a vine did not hold. The torn vine lay right across our path, and the heel mark was deep in the earth. As for the bush, it was less obvious that it had actually been trampled, but the dogs were now sniffing the leaves and giving out little whimpers and yelps.

At first the inspector held the dogs back, but when he gave them a little more rope, they actually began pulling him. With their noses close to the ground, they moved out away from the path and along the edge of the lawn to the trees. There the dogs again became lost, or at least had their attention diverted by a squirrel that fled into the branches above. But once on the other side of the trees, the dogs were out on open land. Fred and the constable, both out of breath, fell behind as the dogs, with their instincts aroused, led the way between thickets of brush and up the sandy inclines.

It has been said that only a storm can bring out the full beauty of nature. Even love, they say, often sleeps until awakened by its opposite. But on this morning, under a perfect blue sky, it seemed wrong that we should be on a hunt amid the flowers, the croaking of insects, and the colorful darting of birds. The place to which the dogs were now headed was the vault we had been excavating. They went straight to the opening of the shaft that Fred and I and his lordship had dug, and then, as they scrambled down inside, the inspector nearly fell on his face as he was pulled in after them.

Inside that dark, dirt-walled room, the dogs soon found a blanket and a pillow, though whoever had used them was gone. The only occupant still in the chamber was a nameless man from the past whose bones lay in chains on the floor.

"What is this place?" asked the inspector.

"It was a temple once," I told him.

"A temple?" asked the inspector. "But why is there this skeleton?"

The inspector let the dogs tear at the blanket and pillow, while he himself bent down over the bones.

"Most likely, or so his lordship believes, it was a temple of Mithra," I said. "Mithra was a god of the Persians and was popular among Roman troops. There are many pagan temples in England. Paganism found the ground fertile here."

"But this skeleton," said the inspector. "Why is this skeleton in chains?"

"It was a mystery religion," I told him, "and the secret of the chained skeleton was known only to the initiated. Perhaps it was not unlike the cross that you see in Christian churches today. Or, as some scholars believe, the chained skeleton may have been a symbol of how the soul is enchained in the flesh and only in death can be freed."

"Good Lord," said Inspector Bland.

When the inspector said this, I thought he was reacting to what I had told him. But it seemed he had just realized that the dogs were loose and had run outside again. Susan and the inspector and I followed, and outside we found them in pursuit of a figure who was attempting to run. The runner fell. The dogs were almost upon him when he scrambled back to his feet. He went over a rise, disappeared from our sight, and then was seen as he climbed the next hill.

On the other side of that hill there was a spring where the dogs would not follow. The young man's clothing was torn. There were scrapes on his elbows and knees. But he was able to wade into the water where he was safe until the dogs were roped up. "Are you," the inspector asked him, "the Timothy Staughton who calls himself Loft?"

"I am," the young man admitted.

"Then you are under arrest," said the inspector. "You already know the charge of robbery against you, but added to it is something far more serious. After further investigation, you may be charged with the crime of murder."

I thought Susan might be about to faint. But as she sighed, her young lover stepped forward and she fell into his arms. It was as perfect a meeting as one could ever see on a stage.

Seventeen

*C*lear as the sky may have been, an ill wind was blowing through Marley; for it was on the very day of this arrest that I received a message from Lord Tigraines. Wreckage from the yacht had been found, and I was asked to proceed at once to Dublin, where his lordship would be waiting for me.

I could not, of course, leave until the next morning, by which time Timothy Loft's situation appeared only to be worse. The townspeople were in a state of excitement, as several different versions were told of the circumstances of Timothy's arrest. The account that I have presented, and that was based on my own observations, was contradicted by the tale of how the young man, surprised in his lair, had fought tooth and nail before capture. Someone was even to claim that he had kicked one of the dogs in the face, causing it serious injury.

There was also the spectacle, it is true, of Susan's riding with her friend to the jail. She clung to him even when he was handcuffed, which should have stirred those hearts moved by romance. But although the young man was handsome, this did not bring him much sympathy. People were now speaking of prowlers whom they had heard in the night. Missing items, many lost for some time, at last had their disappearance explained. After all, as I heard people saying, the young man had been in Marley before. He had passed through with the theatrical troupe, and it was remembered that at that time a widow, old Mrs. Marvel, had died mysteriously in her sleep.

Sam Shakespeare, who was at the station when I boarded the train that next day, said to me: "Just think, George, it was your theory that the young man was at fault. That was the way, when Susan was arrested, that you thought her name could be cleared."

"Yes, I know," I said to him. "I was wrong. The young man is equally innocent."

On the train at least I was alone, so that I could review the case in my mind and even bring these notes up-to-date. But once in Holyhead, where I boarded the boat, I was to be on the dark, churning sea where Sir Michael and Lady Mary had drowned. After that all my thoughts were of them, and of the man I would be meeting in Dublin as soon as the boat reached the shore.

I had never seen him the way he was then, for his lordship's face had a gray, ashen look, which together with the black clothes he wore gave him a kind of spectral appearance. Though people had often said of Lord Tigraines that he did not look like an Englishman, I had never been sure what they meant. Certainly it was nothing so simple as that he looked Italian or French. But that day I not only had a feeling he did not look English; he hardly seemed human at all.

On the drive north neither of us said much. And when his lordship did try to speak, his voice had a strange, reedy sound, as if in the searching at sea he had contracted some disease of the lungs. "George," he said, "I suppose you will want to know what happened."

"Not now," I told him. "We can speak of it later."

"Yes," he said, "perhaps that would be better. But the truth is that very little is known. They were planning to sail to an island where there are ruins of an old hermitage. Sir Michael liked to explore those ruins and had been there many times before. It was a storm, which came without warning, that must have blown them off course. We found, after nine days of searching, only part of a mast and a sail."

"It was a terrible accident," I said. "Everyone in Marley feels the loss. The vicar is calling a service especially to pray for their souls."

"Their souls," his lordship said sadly. "I have never known what a soul is, George, and I have never really believed in prayer. But it is good that the vicar should do this and that the people of the town should attend."

"They all remember Lady Mary," I told him. "She must have been remarkable as a girl."

"Yes, and now there is her daughter," said his lordship. "That is the real reason I called you here. We will be returning to Longmoor with Ethel. I suppose she is Lady Ethel now."

The estate where the McNaughts had lived was far smaller than I had expected. Actually, it was little more than a farm with a sloping pasture that led down to the sea and an enclosure for a small flock of sheep. The house itself was built of stones from the coast and these stones were now so covered with moss that from a distance the building looked green.

Little Ethel appeared unaware of the tragedy of what had occurred. When we arrived, she was out with the sheep and came running to the house in excitement. "Uncle Alfred, who is it?" she called. For a moment, from the look on her face, I had the feeling she thought I was her father. Perhaps the reason for this was the sun, which was just low enough at that time to have blinded her eyes to my face. But then she saw, I think with disappointment, that I was a man with two arms.

"I have brought you a present," said his lordship, holding out a package to her. "And I have come with the friend, Mr. Howard, whom I told you about yesterday."

The girl, as she accepted the package, looked at me with an expression of puzzlement. "Are you the man from America?" she asked.

"Yes," I said.

"Then do you know Natty Bumppo?" she asked. "Have you ever met Chingachgook?"

I shook my head.

"My father read me a book about them," she said. "It is called *The Last of the Mohicans*."

The girl had to go back to the sheep because some of them, drifting apart from the others, were wandering too close to the shore. Lord Tigraines and I watched for a moment as she pulled one of them back, causing the others to follow. Then his lordship took me into the house, where I was introduced to the housekeeper who had been taking care of the girl.

"She is a good child, Mr. Howard," said this woman. "But the day will come when she awakens and knows her parents will never return. When that day comes, I do not wish to be there. I have seen too many deaths in this country, and too many children in tears."

The girl, we could see from a window, was unwrapping the gift from his lordship, which turned out to be a music box. The tinkling notes, faint in the distance, were those of an old lullaby.

Lord Tigraines had no interest, it seemed, in staying on in Ireland. Now that the search had been ended, he arranged to have the sheep sold to a farmer and the old house boarded up. It was the selling of the sheep that seemed most to disturb the girl, but she was also curious about where she was going.

"Is Longmoor in America?" she asked me.

"Longmoor is in England," I told her. "People say that in the time of Queen Igraine it was even a castle."

"But Queen Igraine," she said, "was the mother of King Arthur."

"Yes," I said, "so the legends tell us."

She stared as if it was the first time in her life that the ancient lineage of her family had even been hinted to her. "Will I be living in this castle?" she asked.

"It is not really a castle," I told her. "It is only an English estate. But yes, you will be living in it."

There was a pause, and she seemed to be thinking. Then she said: "When I am living in this castle, will my mother and father be there?"

"Your mother and father," I answered, "will be living with you all your life."

It may have been wrong of me to say this. Sometimes, when one is talking to children, one says things, in order to comfort them, that one knows will be misunderstood. What I meant, and probably should have said, was that their memory would always live with her. But she did not ask for an explanation and did not mention the matter again until we were actually on our way, crossing the sea to England. At that time, as his lordship and I were standing with her at the rail, she asked her uncle if what I had said was true. Lord Tigraines looked at me for a moment. Then he nodded and patted her on the head.

Eighteen

During the time we were in Ireland, I did not want to trouble his lordship with the problems of Timothy Loft. I did, of course, mention the fact that the young man had been arrested, and was thought to be a thief; but it was only after we had boarded the train that Lord Tigraines raised the issue himself.

"You had better tell me a little more," he said then, as the train raced through the Welsh countryside. "Who exactly is this Timothy Loft whom our Susan seems to be in love with?"

"His name is Staughton rather than Loft," I said. "Like Susan, he changed his name for the stage, and he is actually a rather handsome young man. He has that look of emerging manhood, which to a woman may be as interesting as emerging womanhood is to a man."

His lordship glanced at his niece, who had placed the music box on the seat and appeared not to be paying attention. "I see," he said, "but there must be something else. If he was in the acting troupe, do you remember having seen him yourself when you took Susan and the others to the play?"

"Now that you mention it, I certainly do," I said. "I had not thought about it before, but I do remember a rather awkward young man whom I recognized in more than one role. In one scene he was old, in the next young. It was totally unconvincing."

"Then he was not," said his lordship, "what you would call a good actor."

"Exactly the opposite," I said. "People in the audience always laughed when they saw him."

"At least that is encouraging," said his lordship.

"Encouraging?" I asked. "In what way?"

"Merely in the fact," said his lordship, "that if he was not a good actor, our Susan was less likely to be fooled. We do still have the problem of the thefts. A cashbox was stolen from the troupe, as well as possibly other objects in town. Were these objects stolen during a performance?"

"I do not know," I said.

"That is something to find out," he told me. "If they were stolen during a performance, or only found to be missing afterwards, then very possibly what the thief did was to take advantage of the fact that his victims were attending the play. Certainly no actor could do that, and particularly not one who had to keep changing costumes in order to appear in each scene. The one most likely to be guilty would be the person who was selling the tickets and did not have to go on the stage."

"He would be the same one who was in charge of the cashbox," I said, "so that he could be guilty of that crime, too."

"That would certainly be my opinion," said his lordship, "but as to whether or not it is correct, we will have to let a court decide."

His lordship, in this exercise of the mind, seemed to have recovered somewhat from the melancholy of his grief. I was anxious for him to go on and explore, in a similar way, the more complicated life of Sir James. But he disappointed me by reaching into his pocket and drawing out a little book he had brought. It was Lucian's *Dialogues of the Gods*; and though occasionally I could see his lips smile at this greatest of all satirists, for the most part his face remained grave. I even wondered how much he was reading, since he would stare at one page, then the next, with his eyes hardly moving at all.

"By the way," I said to him at last, "when Sam and I were on the train leaving London, we shared a compartment with someone you might remember. She and her husband met you in Athens when they were on their honeymoon."

"At the Acropolis, you must mean," said his lordship, closing the little book in his hands.

"Yes," I said, "the woman's husband taught Greek. You must have made a good impression on him, since he said you were the best student he ever had."

"Old C. H. Fathergill," said his lordship, "used to say that about all his students. He was almost ready to retire when he married, but I remember his wife was quite young. There was something odd about her, though. As I recall, she wore a very strange hat."

"A hat with feathers?" I asked.

"Not just feathers," said his lordship. "It seemed to have wings on each side."

"Like the cap of Hermes," I suggested.

"Yes," he said. "Is she still wearing it?"

"I do not see how it could be the same one," I told him, "but there were certainly feathers on her hat. She kept adjusting them on the seat at her side. And there was something else that she told us, too, though I do not know if it is proper to repeat it."

"You are an American, George," said his lordship. "Everything is proper to you."

"Yes, it is proper," said little Ethel, whose curiosity appeared to have been aroused.

"Well, what she told us," I said, "was that when her husband introduced you, he called you by a kind of nickname. He did not call you Lord Tigraines, but Lord Tiger."

"Is my uncle a tiger?" asked little Ethel.

"He was called that as a young man," I told her, "and he is probably embarrassed by it now."

"On the contrary," said his lordship. "It was a name in which I always took pride."

"I will call you Uncle Tiger then," said the girl.

Lord Tigraines, who had only smiled at great Lucian, was now actually to laugh out loud. "You may call me anything you like," he told her, "just so long as Mr. Howard and myself are the only ones who hear you."

It was clear that both his lordship and I were beginning to find pleasure in the company of this girl. But in the case of his lordship, of course, there may have been the added awareness that the niece was his sister reborn. "Now, George," his lordship said to me, "the time has come to hear what you have learned about the death of Sir James. With young Timothy under arrest, is it your feeling that the case has been solved?"

"Not at all," I said.

"Then has your mind changed?" he asked. "I seem to remember that in one of your letters you expressed the idea that he might be guilty."

"That was before he was captured," I said. "Now I am in agreement with you that he is innocent both of the murder and very likely of the robbery charge. He was seen, of course, by Miss Partridge, as he was fleeing from the scene of the crime. But that is the only evidence against him."

"That evidence is in his favor," said his lordship. "If he did not leave what you call the scene of the crime until the morning when Sir James was found, then he must not have known what had happened. The discovery of Sir James on the stairs must have come as a surprise to him, too."

"And as such a surprise," I added, "that he left some of his clothing behind."

"That is exactly right," said his lordship. "What we must try to determine is who else might have been in the house that night. I understand, from reports of the inquest, that there was a bottle of wine."

"It was an empty bottle that Susan washed," I said. "She wanted to make it into a vase."

"So she explained," said his lordship. "But sometimes such a bottle indicates that a person has had guests."

"Yes," I said, "but we have no idea who the guests could have been. There was a letter that Sir James left unfinished, but it seems to have been meant for the vicar."

"Was this letter to the vicar," asked his lordship, "the only writing found among his effects?"

"It was the only writing done just before his death," I said, "and we cannot be sure it was intended for the vicar. That is only the way it appears."

"I see," said his lordship. "Then was there something else, too, some other writing that was not quite so recent?"

"There was a journal," I told him, "but unfortunately it is no help. It is just a workbook that Sir James kept in the field."

His lordship again opened the Lucian. "As I indicated in my letter," he said, "I have done some investigating myself, and when we get back I will ask the constable if I can see this journal. Also, though the bottle was washed, I doubt very much that the cork was. I will ask if the cork has been found, and if it has been analyzed."

Lord Tigraines turned a page in the book, after which he resumed his reading.

Nineteen

When we arrived in Marley, there was more than the usual ceremony attendant on the lord's return. Lord Tigraines, as the ancients advised, had always wished to live in obscurity. But he did not. He could not be obscure, and particularly not when the whole town had been informed of his train's arrival. Half the village was at the station to greet him, and the other half we found lining the road on the drive out to Longmoor.

The townspeople, along with the servants, were dressed in black on that day; and his lordship, at the sight of these people, had to turn his face away. "They are not honoring me," he told Ethel, "but the memory of your father and mother, whom they always held in respect."

Ethel by then understood. Though she said nothing, her eyes became red, and she had to keep wiping the corners with the little handkerchief in her hand. At Longmoor it was Susan who presented flowers to the girl, just as she had once, years before, presented them to his lordship. Then Ethel, as she looked at the house and at all the servants standing in front, said to me: "But it is a castle."

And so it seemed on that tragic homecoming. The turrets, with their ancestral flags, had been draped in the black of mourning. Except for Ethel's bouquet of flowers—the brightest blossoms from the trees and the fields—everything appeared covered in gloom. One knew then how it had been in the past when, after sieges and plagues, there had been similar times of grief. Even the sky, gray in the late afternoon, had that somber look of doom that must once have hung over Hastings and over the battlements of old Camelot. But then suddenly, through a break in the clouds, a shaft of sunlight, like a long gleaming sword, turned the windows of the house into gold. Ethel, clutching the flowers in one hand, put her other hand in her uncle's. Together they went up the steps.

In those first days at Longmoor his lordship made no engagements. Occasionally there would be visitors, but Lord Tigraines rarely received them. He did receive the vicar, of course, and he also talked to the constable. But Inspector Bland had gone back to London, and his lordship was even to appear bored with the case the constable presented. His lordship did inquire about the cork, which the constable said he would look for; and he also made the request that he be allowed to read Sir James' journal. But the journal, when it arrived, was merely left on a table in the library. In the evenings, when his lordship and I would share what he called the last cup of truth, I would find him reading Philostratus, or perhaps the essays of Montaigne.

It seemed that the only thing, in those days, that could lift his lordship's mind from his loss was the presence of his little niece. Ethel needed a governess and a tutor; and while for the second position he chose himself, the first appeared harder to fill. "Go see Fred," said his lordship one day. "Tell him to send Susan to me."

I went to the gardener's cottage, and when I informed Fred of his lordship's request, he was worried about what it might mean. "My daughter has been a good girl," he said. "I am teaching her to help with the flowers, and she is showing that she has the right touch. Nature asks only for kindness, which it then gives in return."

"His lordship is kind, too," I told him. "I am sure that

whatever it is that he wants to see Susan about, it will be for her benefit."

Susan, as we went to the house, was as apprehensive as her father. "Lord Tigraines," she said, "must think me wrong in not speaking against Timothy."

"No," I told her, "whatever it is, I am sure that it could not be that."

Lord Tigraines was waiting for us in the hall, where he towered like a giant above the armor of his ancient ancestors. For one of the few times since his grief, he even appeared to be smiling. "I do not imagine," he told Susan, "that you are aware yet of why I called you here."

"I do not know," Susan said, "but I hope your lordship is not angry with me. There is an explanation for everything I have done."

"You have nothing to explain," said his lordship. "Mr. Howard, who is your champion, has already made it quite plain that you are totally innocent. Of course, you did deceive the police when you helped hide your friend, but that is their problem, not mine. If I have any objection myself, it is only with regard to the fact that you seem not to trust me."

"Not trust your lordship?" said Susan.

"With your name," said Lord Tigraines. "You still call yourself Quint, or Quintleigh, when I believe your true name is now Staughton—or Loft, if that is what you prefer."

I was as startled as I think Susan was when Lord Tigraines spoke. Somehow, in my concern for her, I had never thought that part of this concern, regarding what the vicar might have called the state of sin she seemed to have lived in, had never been necessary at all. "Yes," said Susan though in my excitement I could hardly hear her voice.

"Does your father know?" Lord Tigraines asked.

"He knows," she said, "but we have kept it a secret. We did not think your lordship would approve of the wife of an accused criminal."

"On the contrary," said Lord Tigraines, "I see no problem with that at all. The difficulty we now have in this household is that my niece has been orphaned and will need a governess. I will expect this governess to read to her, and therefore, with your theatrical training, I believe you will be well qualified."

"Qualified as a governess?" Susan asked.

"Most certainly, if you do not object," said his lordship, "and if it meets with the approval of my niece."

After Susan had gone, I asked Lord Tigraines when it was that he had first known she was married, and he told me he had suspected it from the time when she first went away.

"You must feel relieved then," I said, "that your suspicions have been confirmed."

The look of sadness returned to his features. "For Susan's sake I do, George," he answered. "Also her father must be pleased. But there are many without such good fortune, and they should not be condemned. Consider, for example, Erasmus who taught the people of his time how to laugh. If the parents of Erasmus had been married, the progress of thought might have stopped. Had Erasmus not been brought up by a woman who suffered scorn and a plague, do you think he would have had the same courage to stand alone as he did, a little man with a pen in his hand, fighting the forces of hate?"

The choice of Susan as a governess was a surprise to many people in town, but there was never any question of Ethel's approval of her. After all, Susan had given her the flowers; and although Susan was older, the two shared a similar spirit that would soon have them out in the fields, chasing rabbits and catching butterflies that his lordship always made them set free.

At first I think Susan felt awed by the responsibility of her task. As they were becoming acquainted, she would call her charge "your ladyship," which Ethel thought was a term of reproach; and she could never discipline Ethel any more than I could myself. When the time came for this to be done, we sent the girl to the library, where his lordship shut us out.

Lord Tigraines, as his niece's tutor, had to accommodate himself to the fact that so far she had not been brought up as he and his sister had been. Jeremy Bentham, though perhaps not Rousseau, would undoubtedly have been displeased, since little Ethel seemed to know more of sheep than of Latin and geometry. She was a bright child who could be sharp in her questions, and in some of the comments she made; but his lordship felt there was no time to lose in starting her on a new track. That was the reason he sent me to London to buy exercise books, atlases, and a Gramophone with whatever recordings I thought would help train the girl's ear.

Twenty

On my journey to London I also carried three messages. Two of these were for friends of his lordship whom he was inviting to Longmoor for a visit, but the third was for a Mr. Evander Poole whom I had never heard of before. Lord Tigraines had been very specific that this letter should be delivered in person; and when I arrived at the address, which was in a lane near the Smithfield Market, I proceeded to attempt to do this.

The first door I knocked on was opened by a woman who called herself Madam East. She told fortunes and diagnosed illnesses, but she had been there for only a year and had never heard of Mr. Poole. Other doors were not opened, and after going all the way to the garret, where a note said that a Mr. Jonathan Chopin was out giving music lessons, I went back downstairs to the street. I was about to give up altogether when a woman in a tobacco shop came out to sweep the sidewalk. "Are you looking for someone?" she asked.

"Yes," I said, "for a Mr. Evander Poole."

"Well, you will not find him here," she told me. "Mr. Poole has not lived here for six years."

"Then at least he did live here once," I said. "Where did he go, if you do not mind my asking?"

The woman, leaning on her broom, looked at me as if undecided. Then she said: "He went to one of those places where no Englishman rightly belongs."

"What sort of place is that?" I asked.

"One of those countries," she said, "that is not even in the Empire. He had a friend, a man I liked at first, who had one of those nice-sounding names. Yes, his friend was named Deer, I think."

"Was that spelled like the animal?" I asked, preparing to make a note.

"No," she said, "I am wrong. His name was something else. It was Hart. I like people with that sort of name, and he seemed like a nice gentleman."

"You must be talking about Sir James Hart," I told her.

"Sir James?" she said. "You mean he was a knight? No, I am sure he was not that. He was a gentleman, but not a 'Sir.' To me and to Mr. Poole he was always just Mr. Hart, which I thought fitting at first."

"At first but not later?" I asked. "Did something happen to change your mind about him?"

The woman was looking at me again. "I do not want you to think," she said, "that I am a teller of tales. To me a person, man or woman, has a right to privacy. But since you ask, there were two things that happened. One was that this Mr. Hart took Mr. Poole away with him. The other was that there was a woman."

"Was there a quarrel over this woman?" I asked.

"I cannot pretend," she told me, "to know what happens behind people's doors. I know only what happens outside, or when customers come in my shop. But I did hear them talking once, and the woman was extremely angry."

"Was she angry at Mr. Poole?" I asked.

"No," said the woman, "at Mr. Hart. Mr. Hart kept saying, 'Please, Norma, please.' He did not like to have her make such a scene."

"Are you sure her name was Norma?" I asked.

"He called her that," said the woman. "Yes, I am sure that he did."

"Then please go on," I said. "Did you ever find out why this Norma was so angry at him?"

"She did not want Mr. Hart to go away," said the woman. "But I could not blame him for that. Norma was a witch. I will never forget that high, screeching voice that she had. Later I saw her again, but it was from the top of a bus. She was two blocks away, but I would have known that witch's face anywhere."

"About this country where Mr. Poole went," I asked, "do you remember if it was in the Middle East?"

"You mean in the Holy Land?" she said. "No, I am sure it was not there. It was one of those South American countries."

"Was it Paraguay?" I asked.

"That was it," said the woman. "Mr. Hart was one of those mining people, which was another reason, when I found that out, that I no longer liked him. I had a brother who worked in a mine, and they made him go into places so narrow that he could not turn around. When my brother died, they pulled him out by the feet."

"I am sorry to hear that," I said.

"He was a good man, my brother," said the woman. "He never had the sort of education that a fancy person like Mr. Hart had, but my brother used to like to read books. When he was a boy, he even wrote poetry. There was a writer he liked, Mr. Swinburne."

"Algernon Swinburne was a good writer," I said.

"Yes," said the woman, "he was very romantic. My brother never paid attention to girls, but he wrote a letter to Mr. Swinburne. He sent Mr. Swinburne one of his poems, and Mr. Swinburne wrote back. He sent my brother a poem of his own. When my brother went off to the mines, he said he was going to write about the miners. He thought people should know of those men who spent their lives under the ground. 'The toilers in Hades,' he called them. That was going to be the title of his book."

"Did your brother ever write it?" I asked.

"No one knows," said the woman. "When he died the owners of the mine were the first ones to go to his room, and they swore there was nothing in it except some old clothes and a pen. Even the poem from Mr. Swinburne was gone."

"That is certainly terrible," I said, as the woman was wiping her face. "Your brother does, as you say, sound as if he was a good man."

"And you sound like an American," she said. "I never liked Americans very much. They always seem to think they know everything. But maybe you have been living here for a while."

"Yes, I have lived here for a long time," I said. "I almost feel like an Englishman now."

"And you almost talk like one," she said. "There are only a few things in your voice that give away your origin. I would almost think, from the manners you have, that you were a member of the nobility."

"I am not a member of it myself," I told her, "but I do work for someone who is. He is the one who wants to know about Mr. Poole."

"Who is that?" she asked. "Who wants to know?"

"Lord Tigraines," I said.

The woman threw down her broom. "You mean you work for Lord Tiger?" she asked. "A lot of people I know believe he is the greatest man in England. What would he be wanting with Mr. Poole?"

"I am not sure that I can explain that," I said, "but it has to do with something that he and I are working on."

"Then I am sorry I cannot help you," she said, "but Mr. Poole has not been here for years. He never even came back for the things that I have been keeping for him."

"That does not matter," I told her. "You have been a great help anyway."

"Have I?" she asked.

"Yes," I said. "Lord Tigraines will be pleased."

I started away, but the woman called me back. "Wait," she said, "I was just thinking something. If you are American and work for his lordship, that means you must be Mr. Howard. I always wondered what you would look like."

"I hope you are not disappointed," I said.

"How could I ever be that?" she asked. "It is true that you are not as tall as I thought, but there is no one as tall as his lordship, or who has a face quite like his. You tell his lordship, when you see him, that he should marry that nice Lady Catherine, even if she does have a sharp chin. She is a nurse like his lordship's late sister. When he gets old, she can take care of him. But, oh, it was terrible news when we learned that Lady Mary was drowned. I cried when I heard that about her, and about her brave husband, Sir Michael. Yes, you tell your Lord Tiger that it is time he forgot the first ladyship and found some other woman to marry. There are plenty of woman in England, and there would even be myself if I were a little younger and had the right sort of title for him."

Twenty-one

When I returned to Longmoor with the Gramophone and the books, I also, of course, still had the message that Lord Tigraines had written to Mr. Poole. I gave it to him as he sat by the fire in an alcove just off the main hall. "Well," he said, as he tossed it into the flames, "I suppose that part of your trip was wasted."

"You may think that if you like," I told Lord Tigraines, "but I consider it a success. Mr. Poole might not be living at the address you put on the envelope, but I know now why you put it there."

"Is that so, George?" said his lordship.

"Yes," I said, "I know who he is, and I know a great many things about him, as well as about his friend Mr. Hart."

"Mr. Graham Hart, I suppose you mean," said his lordship. "You found out he was a friend of Sir James' brother."

"Yes," I said, "and that he went to Paraguay with him, as I am sure you must have known yourself."

"I knew they were both there," said his lordship, "but it was unclear how that came about, or exactly what their relationship may have been. My information came from a friend who was once a consul in Paraguay, and who only knew the men there. He did supply me with Mr. Poole's old address, but with little other firm information."

"Well, I have that now," I told him. "One of Mr. Poole's former neighbors, a woman who runs a tobacco shop, was personally acquainted with him. I even have the answer to something that was puzzling Inspector Bland, and that I made a mistake on myself."

"Please go on then," said his lordship. "I would like to hear about it."

"It is about something in Sir James' journal," I said. "In that journal, the inspector told me, there is mention of someone referred to as N."

"Not only in the journal," said his lordship. "There is a far bolder reference in the dedication to *The Triumph of Nimrod*. 'To N.,' it says, 'who has made me a hunter, seeking what cannot be found.' "

"Maybe so," I said. "I did not know that, but I can tell you the mistake that I made was in thinking the N referred to Nimrod. Had I known about the dedication, I might have been even more sure of this, since in the Bible Nimrod is called a hunter, too. He is called a mighty hunter before the Lord. But that has nothing to do with the N that Sir James was referring to. His N was a woman named Norma, and Norma was Mr. Graham Hart's wife."

"How did you come to that conclusion?" asked his lordship.

"It was all explained at the inquest," I said. "Susan told us in her testimony that Sir James' brother married the woman whom Sir James wanted to marry himself. Susan did not give us her name. The tobacco lady did that, and then the two pieces fitted together."

"Indeed they did," said his lordship. "I am grateful that you found that out. What else do you know about her?"

"I do not know this for a fact," I said, "but I think the choice the woman made was the wrong one. She and Graham Hart did not get along, though that was probably as much her fault as his. I was told that she was a witch."

"Were you given any indication," asked his lordship, "that she might have recognized her mistake and wished that she had married Sir James instead?"

"No," I said, "I am sure the woman I talked to would not have known about that. She was not really a prying person, but just happened to hear them talking. Later the woman saw Norma again, but it was only from the top of a bus."

"Was Norma alone at that time?" asked his lordship.

"I did not ask," I said. "She was seen from two blocks away, and so it might have been hard to tell."

Lord Tigraines, who rarely showed disappointment, seemed disappointed at this. "All right," he said, "but what about Mr. Poole? What did you learn about him?"

"Just what I have told you," I answered, "and also that he never came back to get the things he left behind."

"Did the woman think he was coming back?" asked his lordship.

"I did not ask," I said. "Do you think he might be dead?"

"Mr. Poole was reported to be dead," said his lordship, "but then later it was thought he was seen. In France it was a great mystery."

"What was Mr. Poole doing in France?" I asked.

"He was on the ship with Sir James," said his lordship. "They were in the same lifeboat together, when the ship broke apart in a storm."

"Then it seems he knew both the brothers," I said.

"It would certainly appear so," said his lordship. "Mr. Poole, I was informed in London, was the one who paid Sir James' ransom after the second kidnapping. Was there anything in what the woman said that would have led you to suspect such a thing?"

"No," I said, "I do not think she knew anything about Graham Hart's brother. When she first mentioned someone named Hart, I even asked her if she meant Sir James."

"What did she say?" asked his lordship.

"She did not think he was a knight," I said.

After that Lord Tigraines asked to know everything that the woman had said, and soon I was explaining about the woman's own brother and the things he was planning to write at the time of his death in a mine. I did not feel it was necessary to mention what had pertained only to me, but I did give his lordship the message that the woman wanted delivered to him. "She called you Lord Tiger," I told him, "just as the lady did on the train."

His lordship, who now poked at the coals, said to me: "I cannot understand, George, why it has taken you so long to learn this, but there are many people in England who still call me by that name. If you attended more of the sessions of our august House of Lords, you would even hear it thrown at me there."

I had known this for some time, of course, but had always felt I should be cautious before actually mentioning it to him. And there was something else I was also cautious about. It was only later, when we went in to dinner, that I asked during the course of the meal if his lordship had ever had occasion to meet the poet Swinburne himself. Lord Tigraines replied that they had met many times, since they had once belonged to the same club.

"Then did he ever say anything to you," I asked, "about a miner or a young man like that who sent a poem to him?"

"No, I cannot say he did," answered his lordship. "But I am sure, if such a poem was sent, that he would have been interested."

Twenty-two

*T*he guests his lordship had invited did not arrive until the following week; but the first to come, Lady Catherine, was already there on the day that a witness was brought into town to testify against Timothy Loft. This witness, a Mrs. Veronne, came all the way from the city of York. The wife of a former seaman, she was the one at whose house Susan lived while Timothy was in custody there. She had seen a prowler, or so she claimed, on the very night of his escape. Among the objects that she had reported missing were a pair of French candlesticks, an ivory carving of the Buddha, and a necklace of pearls from Japan. Since her husband no longer went to sea, the woman said the Buddha and pearls were things she could never replace.

The constable did not, of course, let the woman confront the suspect alone. Instead a group of six was presented, and these included myself, the coroner, and Sam Shakespeare. For a moment, when the woman first saw us, I thought the coroner was the one she would pick. But as she started to point in his direction, the constable said: "Now remember, Mrs. Veronne, it was dark when you saw the prowler, and people often look different in light. Perhaps you would have an easier time if the curtains were drawn in the room."

As the constable darkened the room, a new look came over the woman's face and she was staring directly at me. "There he is," she said, raising a finger. "I would know him anywhere."

"The man you are pointing to," said the constable, "is not the one we hoped you would choose. He is Mr. Howard, Lord Tigraines' secretary, and someone we could hardly suspect of committing this sort of crime."

"You mean he is not a criminal?" asked the woman, who must have thought we were all criminals.

"No, he is not," Ravenwood answered, as he drew back the curtains again.

"Oh, in the light I see differently," said the witness. "I see now he could not be the one. The one who did it is that man over there."

This time she pointed to a person standing so close to Timothy Loft that I thought she might have meant him. But she did not; it was Sam Shakespeare now who she thought was the culprit. Constable Ravenwood had no choice after that but to let Timothy go back to his cell; and when I returned to Longmoor, where his lordship and Lady Catherine were engaged in a game of croquet, I was able to announce that at least one of the charges against Timothy had been dropped.

"Do you know what I think?" I said to Lord Tigraines. "I suspect that there was never a burglar and that the woman made the whole robbery up."

"For what purpose would she have done that?" he asked, as his ball, struck a little too lightly, stopped just short of the wicket.

"In order to conceal from her husband," I answered, "the fact that she had sold the objects herself."

"Did she seem to be that kind of person?" asked his lordship.

"I could not tell," I told him, "what kind of person she was. In the beginning I thought she seemed hesitant, but when she pointed at me and Sam Shakespeare, she appeared very sure of herself."

His lordship's ball, resting in front of the wicket, was blasted off by Lady Catherine's. He had to go into the trees to retrieve it, and by the time he had it back in position, Lady Catherine was two wickets ahead. "She may have been pointing at you," said his lordship, "but I think you should be careful before you point back at her. Even if the objects were not really stolen, there is another explanation both for their disappearance and for her thinking you might have taken them."

"What could that be?" I asked.

"Her husband," said Lord Tigraines. "If her husband was the prowler, he would have been an older man like yourself. She may have seen him in the dark and not known him, since she would not have expected him to be there."

We heard laughter as Susan and Ethel came out on the lawn from the house, and his lordship went on to tell Susan about the good news I had brought. "Your former landlady, Mrs. Veronne," he said, "was unable to identify Timothy as the prowler she saw in her house."

"She identified me," I told her, "and when she learned that I could not have done it, she picked Sam Shakespeare in my place."

"Really? Is that true?" Susan asked. "She thought you and Mr. Shakespeare were guilty?"

"From our appearances, yes," I explained, "but not when she learned who we were."

"And so you see from that," said his lordship, leaning over his mallet, "how easily a person can be charged with a crime he has not committed. Sometimes I wonder, with our system of justice, if all the guilty may not be innocent."

"But if there is a crime," Susan said, "there must be someone who is guilty of it. There must be someone who stole from the troupe, and there must be someone who killed Sir James."

Lord Tigraines made his shot and it was perfect, although

at the next wicket he missed. "Both of them will be found," he told Susan, "and I assure you they will not be the same. The one who stole the cashbox I suspect, but the killer of Sir James can be known with far more certainty."

"Are you saying you know the killer?" I asked.

"I hope you are not surprised by that," said his lordship.

"Certainly not," I told him, "but if you do, the constable and the inspector should be summoned here at once. Then you can lay out the facts before them."

Lord Tigraines stood and watched Lady Catherine as she hit the post through the first double wickets. "In due course that will be done," he assured me, "but the best thing to do now is to wait. When Timothy Loft goes on trial, he will want his defense to be new. Let people wonder if there is a defense. Let them even think Timothy guilty. They will find, by the end of the trial, that everything has been turned upside down."

"Then you are sure he will be freed?" Susan asked.

"I am as sure of that," said his lordship, "as I am that our friend Mr. Howard never stole from anyone's house." With Lady Catherine four wickets ahead, Lord Tigraines bent down to make his next shot. Then he looked up. "By the way, George," he said, "why not get one of those gold candlesticks that you and I were given in India? If Mrs. Veronne has not left, it might help to make up for her loss."

Mrs. Veronne had not left. I found her waiting for the train at the station; and when she saw what I had brought, she looked at me with even greater suspicion than she had when the curtains were drawn. She bit the candlestick to test its metal, after which she put it under her coat.

Twenty-three

*T*o have Lord Tigraines say, or at least begin to hint, that he knew the killer of Sir James was disconcerting to me at that stage. Naturally, it was not just the police to whom I wanted to have the murder explained; I was anxious to know his lordship's theories myself. When I returned from seeing Mrs. Veronne, he did ask a question of me, but this was only about Sir James' dogs. He wanted to know if they were still at Redland; and I told him no, that it was my understanding that they had been sent to an animal shelter where they would be taken care of.

"Put to sleep, do you mean?" asked his lordship.

"No," I said, "it will be nothing like that. In the shelter they will be fed and cared for, and then trained for duty with the police. Are you thinking they might help with the case?"

"From what I have heard," said his lordship, "they have been of enough help already."

At dinner that night, there was a good deal of talk of Sir James by both Lady Catherine and the other London guest, who had arrived. Lady Catherine, who if she had a sharp chin was also someone with a very sharp mind, said she had developed her own theory on the basis of a detective story she had read. In this story the death had been accidental when a poison, in this case prussic acid, had been mistaken for ordinary sugar and baked as an ingredient in a pie.

"And that was all by accident?" asked his lordship.

"Entirely," said Lady Catherine. "Of course, the pie had an unusual taste, but the victim of the accident had a cold and therefore was not aware of it."

"That is interesting," said his lordship. "I wonder if Sir James had a cold and if he may have heated the wine before proceeding to drink it. There are still a number of problems related to questions such as that, though the general outline is clear."

The general outline, I was about to say, was clear only to his lordship; but then the other guest, a cabinet minister (whose name and ranking I feel I should withhold), made a statement I was not prepared for but that explained in part why he was there. "Sir James," this gentleman said, "was never much of a drinker of wine. If it is found that he had a cold, I think Tigraines may be right that he used it as a medicine."

"You speak," I said to this guest, "as if you had some acquaintance with Sir James."

"I suppose I did," the minister answered. "We were actually quite close at one time. When two Englishmen find themselves in a place where they are surrounded by nomads and sand, it is not unusual for a bond to develop."

"You must have met him in Arabia then," I said.

"It was in Baghdad," said the minister. "I will never forget the first time I saw him. Sir James had been out in the field for so long that his face had been burned almost black. He wore robes, not an Englishman's dress, just as Tigraines did at Mecca. It is always quite a sight to see an Englishman walking through a bazaar with a black face and robes of the desert. Did I say he had been in the field? The truth is that it was a little more than that. He had been captured by bandits who asked a ransom for him. There was no one, really, to pay it except a brother who was not on the scene, and so I helped a little myself. I did not know him, though I had heard of his work; and I was certainly not prepared for the kind of man Sir James turned out to be."

"What sort of man was he?" asked Lady Catherine, clearly as interested in all this as I was.

"He was wild," said the cabinet minister. "Sir James was absolutely insane. You have heard, I suppose, that the desert is a breeding ground for the mad. In ancient times men lived in deserts on pillars, baking their brains in the sun. Sir James was a man on a pillar. Do you know what he said to me when we first met? He said: 'Greetings. I am Spitama.' Truly, I was amazed that this was the man I had ransomed, and I wondered if it had been worth it. Spitama was the name of Zarathustra, the one called Zoroaster by Greeks."

"Did these ravings continue long?" I inquired.

"They continued almost the whole time I knew him," said the cabinet minister. "But that did not prevent our becoming friends. Of course, as you probably found out here, Sir James was a very secretive person, and he did not make friends easily. There was trouble, I was told, at his diggings. His workers, always close to revolt, must have noticed the madness in him."

"The man you are describing," I said, "sounds as if he must have made enemies."

"I suppose that he did," said our guest. "Certainly there were many who did not like him, though a man like that also gains some respect. That was the way he survived with the brigands. If he had been a man to crawl on his knees, begging his captors for mercy, they would have shown how little mercy they had. But he stood up to them and put on the mantle of one of their land's greatest prophets. Zoroaster was no stranger to brigands, or to men who held knives in their hands. For many years he wandered mountains and deserts, before at last, in a temple of fire, he was stabbed from behind by a priest."

"I hope Mazda forgives you," said his lordship.

"What was that?" asked the cabinet minister. "Oh, yes, those were his last words. Zoroaster called on his god, the Lord Mazda, and turning to his attacker, he said: 'May Lord Mazda forgive you as I do.' There was a touch of kindness in Zoroaster. At the end he was like Jesus Christ, who did not live for another six hundred years."

"What was he like with women?" asked Lady Catherine.

"Do you mean Sir James?" said our guest. "Or are you talking about Zoroaster?"

"I suppose either one," said the lady, "since you seem to be saying they were the same."

"I never meant to say that," the man told her. "The truth is that I am not an expert on the question of Zoroaster himself. If he did resemble Sir James, though, then I would say the ladies must have liked him. Women, I have often observed, are very peculiar in these matters. You take the man who dresses up in a suit, even in the hottest climates. Let him put the proper oil on his hair, perfume himself, and have a neat, tweezered beard. Do you think that will impress a woman? Do you think the starch of a collar is what she wants to see on his neck? No, what a woman admires is a man who has dirt on his hands. She likes the savage look of a turban. Let her see the ragged flutter of robes, the flash of eyes from an unshaven face, and the delicate creature will swoon."

"I am swooning already," said Lady Catherine. "Do you mean to say Sir James was such a man?"

"What I mean to say," said the cabinet minister, "is that he cut the kind of figure in Baghdad that few other Englishmen could."

Twenty-four

*L*ord Tigraines was only partly right about everything being turned upside down. When Timothy Loft had his trial, which like the inquest was held in Whitcross, it was impossible for him not to admit that he had escaped from custody. Other charges against him were dismissed, and there was even a moment of drama when Susan again testified. Though her speech was the same as the one she gave at the inquest, rehearsal had not hurt it at all. That last line, "We were beggars, not thieves," actually had the justice of the peace reaching to take a speck from his eye.

As for Timothy's main accuser, the manager of the acting troupe, no action could be taken against him. Though Sam Shakespeare was very effective in showing that it was this man himself who was most likely to have stolen the cashbox, as well as robbed those attending the plays, there was really no firm evidence. In the end, the trial's principal outcome was that Timothy, although released, would be reprimanded by the justice for not putting more trust in the law.

There may have been some who expected that Timothy would also be accused of the murder of Sir James Hart, but this charge was not brought against him. Inspector Bland, who had returned for the trial, explained afterward to reporters that although this other case was progressing, no arrests were presently contemplated. "It may even be," the inspector said with a wink, "that no arrests are ever going to be made."

"Is that because," asked a reporter, "you believe it to have been suicide?"

The inspector, winking again, seemed almost to have developed a twitch. "More and more," he agreed, "that is the conclusion I am coming to reach."

"What about the letter Sir James was writing?" asked the reporter. "It is rumored that at the time of his death Sir James was about to name his killer in a letter."

"That rumor is false," said the inspector. "There was a letter, but it is not of importance. No longer can it be considered to have any bearing on the case."

The reporter doing this questioning was the same man who some weeks before had followed us from the Green Fox. I had thought then that what he had noticed was the crest on the door of his lordship's car, and now he was to ask the inspector about Lord Tigraines' role in the case.

"Lord Tigraines has been very helpful," said the inspector. "I have not talked to him personally, but he has made a number of suggestions, both to the constable and to my superior at the Yard. Naturally, with our normal procedures, we did not have to be told to look for a cork. But nevertheless we appreciate the assistance of those whom, with no disrespect, I shall call amateurs."

"Are you saying," asked the reporter, "that Lord Tigraines is only an amateur?"

"His lordship," the inspector replied, "is of course more than an amateur. He is one of the most eminent men in the kingdom, and has often been described as our country's premier dilettante. But when it comes to a case of this kind, whether it proves to have been a suicide or a murder, it is always best to leave things in the trained hands of professionals. At the present time his lordship has in his possession the journal that was kept by Sir James in the field. He asked to see it, and it was given to him. But now it will have to be taken back. It will be turned over to our experts in London, who will include, let me assure you, specialists in that field of study that is known as psychology. If Sir James did commit suicide, the seeds of it may be found in those notes."

As the inspector was about to get in the car where Ravenwood was waiting for him, the reporter asked one last question: "Will you be seeing Lord Tigraines yourself?"

"Lord Tigraines, as you know," said the inspector, "has been in mourning over the death of his sister. I will be going to Longmoor, of course, for the purpose of retrieving the journal. But whether or not his lordship will be in a mood to receive me, I am in no position to say. I rather suspect, since he was not at the trial, that he might prefer not to see me at all."

I could have told the inspector this was not true. His lordship's not attending the trial was a matter of courtesy to the court. Never, once a case was in court, did he wish to tip the scales of justice by appearing in person.

Twenty-five

When Susan, Timothy, and I returned to Longmoor that day, we found that his lordship was upstairs, listening to the new Gramophone. "He has been there all morning," said Lady Catherine, who was in the garden with the cabinet minister. "I must say some of the music is good, but I much prefer to hear Caruso in person."

It was, in fact, Caruso's voice we heard then, first ascending the high notes of Verdi and then falling into cries of despair. "Bravo," the cabinet minister shouted when this record came to an end, and his shout brought Lord Tigraines to the window.

Lord Tigraines might not have gone to the trial, but he showed a rare happiness at the freedom of Timothy Loft. Coming down into the garden, he shook the startled young man's hand and told the couple they would be welcome at Longmoor for as long as they wanted to stay. "There will not be room in the gardener's cottage," he said. "Instead, I am going to arrange for you to have an apartment in the house. No one has lived in those rooms since I was there on my own honeymoon, and before that, if I remember correctly, they were occupied by a certain Scotsman, John Brown, who shared them with his titled lady."

"Really, Tigraines," said the cabinet minister, "you should not fill these young ears with that. Her late Majesty was the Queen of Decorum. If she needed her servant with her, it was because Brown took care of matters of state."

"And that was exactly what I meant," said his lordship. "It was only out of modesty that I did not name the lady myself."

"You mean Queen Victoria stayed there?" asked Susan.

"She and quite a number of others, if you want the truth," said Lord Tigraines. "I do not carry the list in my head, but you will find it in the guest register, which I very much hope you will sign."

"Your lordship honors us," said Timothy Loft, "but after all that has happened, I think we should visit my father and mother, who have not seen me for a long time."

"That can be done, too," said his lordship. "If you are willing, we can invite them here. But first I must hear of your trial. I am sure my secretary, Mr. Howard, took notes, and so I will ask him to read them."

"My notes are very brief," I told him. "I did not take down everything that was said, but the trial went smoothly, I think."

"How did Shakespeare do?" asked his lordship.

"Sam was absolutely perfect," I said. "He did not quite succeed, naturally, in having Timothy's accuser arrested, but you were right to cast suspicion on him. When Sam said, 'I charge you before this court with having stolen the cashbox yourself,' the man seemed almost to shrink away."

"We will have to invite Sam to dinner," said his lordship. "I did not know he would be quite that forthright. But please go on. What about the murder?"

"That case did not come up," I told him. "The inspector, from what he said later, seems to believe it was a suicide. At least he appears of the opinion that the evidence is pointing in that direction."

"In that event," said his lordship, "we should invite the inspector here, too."

"The inspector is already coming," I said. "He wants to take Sir James' journal back to London, but he did not know if you would receive him."

"Not only will I receive him," said his lordship, "but I will let him explain his theories to us. Who all will be coming so far?"

"Just Sam Shakespeare and the inspector," I said, "unless you are including the rest of us here."

"But I am, of course," said his lordship, "and I would like several others also. Amanda Shakespeare will have to come with her husband, and we will want the constable and his wife. Then there are the Simpsons. Dr. Simpson, after all, was the one who examined Sir James after death."

"What about Mr. Martree, the bookseller?" I asked. "He also tried to be of help in the case."

"Then he should come," said his lordship. "I will let him look at my books. Now how is that? Do you think there are enough?"

"You have left out the vicar," I told him.

"Yes, of course," said his lordship. "We should invite the Hallidays, too. And there is also one other person who I feel ought to be there. I would like Susan to invite her father. If he wishes to know why he should attend, merely say it is a marriage supper, which among other things it will be."

"I know that everyone will be relieved," I said, "that the case is coming to an end. In particular I am sure that the vicar, since he was once under suspicion, will be pleased to learn it was suicide."

"Suicide, you say?" asked his lordship. "Do you mean to tell me that you and the inspector are in agreement on that?"

"It was not my first conclusion," I told him, "but it is one I feel may be warranted now. After all, it is a crime without suspects and without any motive we know."

"I would hardly call it that," said his lordship, "but that is something we can discuss. Tonight, unless I am mistaken, the murderer will be revealed."

In no other case I could recall had his lordship been so melodramatic. "Are you saying," I asked, "that the murderer is someone we know?"

"The murderer of Sir James Hart," said his lordship, "if in truth there was a murderer, will certainly be known to those here."

Twenty-six

After delivering the invitations, I spent the rest of the day going over all the notes I had made. It seemed to me that there must have been something that I had so far overlooked, for his lordship, though my respect for his mind bordered on the worship of genius, had never been a man to leap to conclusions unsupported by the known evidence.

Sitting at my desk before the upper-floor window, I looked down and saw his lordship outside, where he was walking with Lady Catherine and Ethel. I thought perhaps he had received a letter. Something might have come to him from Baghdad, or even from Paraguay. After tea, which was brought to my room, I dressed and went back downstairs, hoping to find his lordship alone. But Lord Tigraines, the cabinet minister, and Lady Catherine were all playing with little Ethel, who enjoyed having an audience. "Here is Mr. Howard," Ethel said when she saw me. "Let us see if he knows who I am."

The game, as Ethel explained it, was a little like that of charades. She was thinking of a famous person and was acting out the part; my job was to guess who it was. I watched as she galloped about the room, but in the end I had to give up. "I am Lady Godiva with her clothes on," she said as the bell rang with the first of our guests.

Mr. Martree was an hour early and had come straight from his shop with a packet under his arm. "I hope his lordship will forgive me," he said, "for descending on him in these clothes, but I really have nothing better to wear."

He was dressed as he always was in his shop—in a jacket with the worn, shabby look of the cover on a secondhand book.

"Lord Tigraines will be pleased to see you," I told him. "He has already made the suggestion that you might want to inspect his library."

"That will be an honor," said Mr. Martree, "and I hope his lordship will also accept these three books as tokens of my esteem."

He held out the packet which I took to his lordship, who let Ethel unwrap it for him. Ethel had trouble with the knots in the string, but at last, with the paper removed, we saw that the three books inside were part of the full set of Lytton that Lord Tigraines already had on his shelves. "It was very kind of you, Mr. Martree," said his lordship, "to have thought of bringing such gifts. Lord Lytton was a favorite of my father and has always been an inspiration to me."

"Do you mean you have these books?" asked Mr. Martree. "Recently I received a set of Plutarch—not the *Lives* but the *Moralia*—that I could have brought for you instead."

"I am afraid," said the cabinet minister, "that if you wish to give his lordship a book, you had better make it one you write yourself. Otherwise, he is bound to have it already."

Mr. Martree had shaken hands with this man, and had even heard me speak his name; but apparently, in his breathless arrival, he had not yet realized who he was. All at once his thin shoulders were trembling. "Oh, my gracious," he said. "I never thought . . . I never would have believed. . . ."

"I am a friend of his lordship," said the cabinet minister, "and do not think of me as anything else. Lord Tigraines may have the books you have brought, but that is only because his ancestors have bequeathed their collection to him. I myself did not have such ancestors. I have only a few books at home; if his lordship does not need these volumes, I would be pleased to accept them in his place."

"You would take them, your grace?" asked Mr. Martree.

"Not as your grace," said the cabinet minister. "I am not in the Church. I am merely an ordinary politician who has sought office through votes such as yours. But yes, I will be happy to take them, so long as you and his lordship approve."

"I not only approve; I insist," said his lordship. "I have always thought you did not read enough. Your speeches are those of a man whose style is derived from newsprint. At least Lytton can elevate that."

The trembling in Mr. Martree's shoulders had not ceased with these pleasantries, and to rescue him from his emotions, I guided him out of the room and into the promised library. There, among the familiar bindings of books, I expected his feelings to calm. But instead, when he saw the high galleries, the packed shelves, and the busts of the great, he seemed almost to go into a faint.

"Good gracious, that is Plato," he said, as if the frown on that face carved in marble was the expression of a still-living mind. "And there," he said, "that must be Seneca."

By far the greatest bust, however, was that of the greatest poet; and the sight of that blind, ancient face nearly brought the man to his knees. For an hour, until the others arrived, he followed me among the shelves where I pointed out to him those books that had always been his lordship's favorites. Mr. Martree told me he knew Lucian and had his own pocket-sized set that he had taken on a trip to Stratford. Also he said he had started to read Philostratus until someone bought it from him.

"The trouble with being a bookseller," he told me, "is that the best ones are taken away, and you get to keep only the worst. You can read, but only in snatches. You learn a little, but never enough."

"No one ever learns enough," I said. "I think even Lord Tigraines would say that. But perhaps we should rejoin the others. Everyone ought to be there by now."

Twenty-seven

When Mr. Martree and I returned to the drawing room, Inspector Bland, who had been the last to arrive, was in the process of repeating the scene that we had had with the bookseller. The inspector, too, was to express amazement at the presence of our distinguished guest. "But I had no idea," he was saying. "No one told me your grace would be here."

"And no one should have," said the cabinet minister. "I am not here on official duties, but merely in order to have a rest."

"Inspector Bland," his lordship commented, "has come highly recommended to us. His superior, Sir Bruce Nottingham, has told me that he was the one who solved the famous Applegate case."

"I read the tapestry," said the inspector, "but that was something any child could have done."

"Modesty has no place here," said his lordship. "You must take credit when it is yours."

"By all means," said the cabinet minister. "You should be proud of a solution like that. I wish others of our inspectors could show ingenuity of that kind. Too often, while crime roams the streets, they sit back merely wringing their hands. I am looking forward, in fact, on this occasion to seeing how you match up with Tigraines, whose talents in these things are well known. Perhaps at one of our cabinet meetings I will even be able to mention that I was present to see you at work."

"I am not here," said the inspector, in command of himself once again, "to make boasts or match wits with a lord. My original purpose in coming was merely to retrieve the journal that his lordship has been allowed to read. If I stay for dinner, I hope it will not mean that I have to explain all the steps that have led to my present conclusions."

"Certainly not," our distinguished guest said. "Such things are like secrets of state. No one would want you to divulge them. But nevertheless, from what his lordship has told us, it appears the crime may have been solved."

"And so it has," the inspector responded. "It remains only for our people in London to put the finishing touches on it. Once a study has been made of the journal, and this done with the most advanced techniques of the science of psychology, it should be possible, beyond the least doubt, to establish why a man like Sir James would have wanted to take his own life."

"I suppose you know," said the cabinet minister, "that I was acquainted with Sir James myself."

"No," said the inspector, "I was not aware of that. Did your grace meet him after he moved to Marley?"

"We met in Baghdad," said the guest. "Of course, it was some years ago; but I must say, from what I knew of him then, that he was someone with a strong will to live. I would even say he was a man with a mission, a Zoroaster as he called himself, who would let nothing stand in his way."

"People change," responded the inspector.

"So they do," said the cabinet minister. "But I just thought, for whatever it might be worth, that I would mention that side of the man. I am sure, when your psychologists read the journal, they will find an explanation for it. They may say this fearlessness that I saw was actually a seeking of death."

"That could well be true," said the inspector. "Many times, in my profession, I have found things to be the opposite of what on the surface they appear."

His lordship, in his role as the host, did not comment on these matters at first. He was friendly to the inspector, but the ones to whom he paid most attention were Mr. Martree and Fred Quint. Susan's father had required coaxing to come, and the only way he could finally be convinced was by being told he could wear his old uniform. He had been a butler earlier in his life, as Susan's mother had once been a maid. Though now he had nothing to serve, nor any duties to perform, he stood like a gray, former soldier called back to review a parade. I could not hear all that his lordship was saying to his gardener and to the dealer in books, but now and then I saw the eyes of the father gazing at his daughter with pride.

Susan and her husband were themselves in a corner, where the vicar, speaking in a loud voice, was informing them and Lady Catherine of the importance of monogamy. "It is our greatest achievement," the vicar was saying, "and the one thing that separates us from the barbarians of the past. Of course, King Solomon did have more, and we hear about the three wives of Moses. But these exceptions were for exceptional men, as I am sure her ladyship will agree."

Her ladyship, the wistful Lady Catherine, certainly must have been in agreement, so long as what the vicar was saying would leave room for a subsequent marriage among gentlemen who had become widowers. After nodding politely in response, Lady Catherine went over to join his lordship, who by then had Mr. Martree explaining about the Jesuits in Paraguay.

I myself joined the Ravenwoods and Shakespeares, and after I had made the comment that I thought the trial had gone well, Tom Ravenwood asked what his lordship now thought about the death of Sir James. My answer was: "I am afraid that is something that Lord Tigraines himself will have to explain."

"I certainly hope he does not try to do it while we are eating," said the constable's wife. "For the longest time now, that is all my husband has had on his mind. He talks of nothing but poison and prowlers."

"In our family it is different," said Amanda Shakespeare. "I cannot get Sam to say anything."

His lordship, though some distance away, apparently heard these remarks; for when the time came to go in to dinner, he was to say to the constable's wife that he hoped the conversation would not upset her digestion. "Oh, no," Mrs. Ravenwood said, "your lordship may say what he likes. I have been hearing so much about poison that I think by now I am immune."

Twenty-eight

After all of us had taken seats at the table, Lord Tigraines began the discussion by talking not about poison, but about the fact that no meat would be served. "I think all of you, except the inspector, are aware of that by now," he said, "and in the past I have always found that my guests were quite willing to accept this restriction."

"I accept it, too," said the inspector, who had been sniffing, as if with suspicion, at the bowl of lentil soup before him. "I worked on a case in which there was a vegetarian once."

"Not the criminal, I hope," said his lordship.

"No," said the inspector, "the victim. He was a man of leisure, like your lordship. It was not necessary for him to keep his mind and body in trim."

"As it is for you, I suppose," said his lordship.

"I am a workingman," the inspector responded. "It is true that I do most of my work with my brain, but the brain needs nourishment like the body. For the brain to function properly, it must be exercised and fed the right food. Without meat, the brain, like other muscles, soon becomes useless and slack."

"If that is your belief," said his lordship, "you must frequently eat meat yourself."

"At every meal," answered the inspector. "Very often it is all that I eat."

"I, too, eat meat," said the cabinet minister, "but not for the same reasons you do. I eat it because it is my habit, and because, except when I am here, it is what people usually serve."

"Your grace owes everything to it," said the inspector. "No one could have risen to such a high place if he had dined only on vegetables."

"That I question," said the distinguished guest. "You are aware, I suppose, that there have been a number of men, far more eminent than any in this room, who have lived on the strictest of diets. That Zoroaster we spoke about earlier lived in the desert on cheese. Then there was Plutarch, whom Mr. Martree mentioned. He also opposed the eating of meat."

"And Seneca," I said.

"Yes, Seneca," said the cabinet minister. "All these men, and many others, were reluctant to see animals die merely to provide them with food. I think they should be respected for that."

"I will respect them," said the inspector, "to the degree such respect is deserved."

"To what degree do you respect the Buddha?" I asked. "How do you feel about Pythagoras, Plato, Epicurus, and Apollonius of Tyana? In Italy there was Leonardo da Vinci. Some consider that eater of vegetables to have been the greatest genius of all. In Switzerland and France were Rosseau, Voltaire, and the historian Michelet. In Germany there was Gustav Von Struve. In Russia there was Count Leo Tolstoy. Even my own country, young as it is, has had the writer Henry David Thoreau, while the vegetarians here in England have included the religious leader John Wesley, the prison reformer John Howard, the poet Shelley, and the playwright Mr. Shaw."

"Mr. Shaw is an Irishman," said the inspector. "I have heard talk of him at the Yard that I would not repeat in this company."

"You are discreet," said the cabinet minister. "Thank goodness you do not repeat things, since it often happens, in a gathering of this kind, that people say what they later regret."

This was the type of conversation that occupied the first part of the meal. All of us, I believe, were waiting for the discussion of Sir James' death to begin, but it was not until the last course, a combination of apples and cheese, that the question was finally raised. "It is my understanding," his lordship said then, "that Scotland Yard believes the case has been solved. I wonder if Inspector Bland would agree to give us the details on it."

"Inspector Bland," the cabinet minister said, "has chosen to use discretion again, exactly as he did with Mr. Shaw. Am I not right, Inspector, that you do not wish to discuss this?"

"Not in full," the inspector said. "Of course not. There are secrets of procedure that I can never divulge. But I think this much can be revealed. It is not Scotland Yard that has solved the case. The conclusions reached so far are my own, and they show, at least to my satisfaction, that Sir James was killed by his own hand."

Lord Tigraines turned to Dr. Simpson. "Would you agree with the inspector?" he asked.

"I have no reason not to," said the doctor. "I am sure he knows the case better than I do. From my own observations, of course, it seemed the victim was taken by surprise. It was not, if you want my opinion, what I would call a passive suicide. The victim, at the end, had been struggling. He was found, after all, on the stairs."

"That is exactly right," said the inspector, "and that was something that threw me off at first, as did the letter he was writing upstairs. But the letter, we now know, was to the vicar. It has nothing to do with the case, except in the fact that it was something unfinished. If you ask why it was unfinished, my answer is that Sir James could not go on. He could not go on with the letter, and he could not go on with his life. He was not certain, or at least not absolutely, that he wanted to commit suicide; and the fact that he was found on the stairs I attribute to a change of his mind. How many of us, on occasion, have thought of jumping off a bridge but turned back? Sir James drank the poison, but then had regret. He fell down before help could be reached."

"That is an interesting theory," said his lordship. "I do not know how many of us have turned back from jumping off a bridge, but on a matter such as that individuals can speak for themselves."

"I was speaking figuratively," explained the inspector. "I wanted to put it in the strongest terms that I could."

"And you succeeded in that," said his lordship. "If I question your solution myself, it is not so much because of what you have told us, but because of what you have left out. Constable Ravenwood was asked about the cork. Did you find the cork to the wine bottle?"

"Yes, we did," the inspector answered.

"And did you have it analyzed?" asked his lordship.

"That was done," the inspector said.

"Then what conclusions did it lead you to?" asked his lordship.

"Only one," said the inspector. "Minute traces of arsenic on the cork confirmed that it was the wine by which the poison was administered."

I glanced over at Mrs. Ravenwood and saw that this mention of poison did not appear to have diminished her appetite. At that moment she was slipping into her mouth a wedge of the apple and cheese. "It seems to me," said his lordship, "that there is another conclusion besides that. If the poison was found on the cork, the wine was poisoned while it was still in the bottle."

"That," the inspector said with a smile, "is something that goes without saying. It was too obvious even to mention."

"It may be obvious as a fact," said his lordship, "but it is not obvious why it was done. Would it not have been a simpler procedure to put the poison straight into the cup, assuming that it was a cup from which Sir James was to drink?"

"Yes," the inspector agreed. "I think we can say that would have been simpler. One often finds, in a case of this kind, that behavior is irrational."

"It would be irrational in a suicide," said his lordship, "but not if there was a murderer."

"And who could such a person be?" asked the inspector. "I am afraid the problem your lordship has in all of this is that none of it proves anything. If your lordship did know the murderer of Sir James, and had any evidence for it, that evidence should be given to the police."

"The case is complicated," said his lordship. "It cannot be explained until its antecedents have been explored."

The inspector's patience seemed to have come to an end. "Never mind the antecedents," he said. "Do you, Lord Alfred Tigraines, know the name of the person who was the murderer of Sir James Hart?"

"If it proves to have been a murder, I most certainly do," said his lordship.

"Then tell us that," said the inspector. "Just tell us the murderer's name. We will know if your lordship could be right."

"The name you are asking for," said his lordship, "is that of his brother, Mr. Graham Hart."

Twenty-nine

At first the inspector appeared stunned; but then, incongruous as it seemed, he gave out a burst of laughter. "His lordship must pardon me," he said. "I hope no one thinks my amusement is a sign of any disrespect. Actually, I should congratulate Lord Tigraines. This very day, at the end of the trial, I was saying to a reporter that the case we are now discussing was not one for an amateur. What I had in mind when I said that, of course, was the sort of armchair detective who solves crimes in the novels these days."

"I understand," the inspector continued, "that there are even some women writers who think they can outdo the men, and outdo the work of professionals. Anyone can dream of this, naturally. I must say I dreamed of it myself before I actually joined the Yard. Once in the Yard, though, I learned things. People say we are slow. Well, we are. Everything we do is step-by-step. We never leap to a conclusion. We never narrow the suspects down to one, or at least not until a case is completed. It is laborious. To a man like his lordship, it might not seem we were detectives at all. To see us at work in the office, some might think we were no more than clerks, shuffling papers back and forth. To see us studying the scene of a crime, some might think we were butlers and servants, cleaning up after one of their balls. But there is method in everything that we do, and that method is meticulousness."

"You have certainly made a very fine statement," said the cabinet minister. "It is the kind of thing that almost deserves framing, as an inspiration to our whole civil service. But you said something at the start that later I found puzzling. You said Lord Tigraines should be congratulated."

"Indeed I did," said the inspector, "and I was about to explain why. Your average armchair detective would not have picked Sir James' brother at all. He would have focused on someone else as the villain, such as the young Timothy here, or the vicar, or Miss Partridge who goes out to watch birds. At the Yard we call these red herrings, since they are the bait for the trap that the amateur quickly falls into. But Lord Tigraines, I discover, did not. His lordship overlooked these people altogether and went after the same person I did. Yes, Lord Tigraines, we were on the same track. We both noticed that Susan here, at the inquest, gave evidence from the victim's own mouth that he and his brother had quarreled."

"As children? Is that what you are saying?" asked the cabinet minister.

"Starting as children," said the inspector. "They were enemies, just like Cain and Abel; and later in life, when Abel became famous, Cain went off to Paraguay. I wrote to Paraguay, as I told Mr. Howard; and then I waited for what I would learn. I cannot blame Lord Tigraines for not having the resources I have, or the contacts in a country like that. But still, I think it would have been wise for his lordship to have been a little more careful. You see, the authorities there have at last responded to my letter. Their reply is right here in my pocket, and I intend to read it to you now. It is not, of course, in the original language, but has been translated at our headquarters, where there are experts in all languages."

"You are certainly giving us an education," said the cabinet minister. "There must be something in your meat after all."

"Do not doubt it," responded the inspector, who had so captured our attention that when he drew the letter from his pocket every fork at the table was still. "Let me quote from this now," he continued, "in the exact words that are written here. 'Dear Scotland Yard,' it begins. 'Your request for information on the whereabouts of Señor Graham Hart has led us to search through our files and discover that the man is deceased. There were several peculiar circumstances surrounding Señor Hart's demise, and if you would like further information, a transcript of our files will be sent.' That is the end of this communication, and naturally I have asked for the transcript, which I am sure will be arriving shortly. We do not have to wait for it, however, to establish this one central fact. Graham Hart could not have killed his brother, because Graham Hart was already dead."

"Well, Tigraines, that certainly sounds conclusive," said the cabinet minister.

"To you, but not to me," said his lordship. "The inspector still does not have the transcript, describing what, as translated by his experts, are called 'peculiar circumstances.' "

"But I suppose your lordship does have it," said the inspector.

"No," said Lord Tigraines, "I do not. But I have spoken to a man who was there. He was a member of our consular corps and had occasion more than once to become acquainted with Graham Hart."

"Rather like my meeting with Sir James," commented the cabinet minister.

"In a sense, but not completely," said his lordship. "While Sir James was a victim of brigands, his brother was a brigand himself. He was not, perhaps, of the type that roams the deserts of the East, but a number of complaints about his behavior were brought to the consular office. I suppose the best way to characterize Graham Hart would be to say he was a confidence man, skilled in the arts of the forger and in those of the alchemist."

"Really, Tigraines," said the cabinet minister. "When you mention alchemy you are going too far. What possible use could it have in this day and age?"

"If your business is mining, a great deal," said his lordship. "But let us not be concerned about that. There is something else that must be mentioned; and that is when the two brothers quarreled, one of these quarrels may have been over a woman. As an indication of the kind of man Graham Hart was, it is interesting that when courted by both, the woman chose him, not Sir James."

"Yes," the inspector said, "we know that. It was all explained at the inquest."

"And it is also in Sir James' journal," said his lordship. "That journal, as anyone can see, combines his search into the past with his dreams, which were related to someone he calls N. Naturally, it might be thought this was Nimrod, about whom Sir James wrote a book. But George Howard, when he was in London, discovered it to be the initial of Norma, the very woman we are now speaking of."

"How did Norma feel?" asked Lady Catherine. "Did she realize she had chosen the wrong brother and afterwards regret her mistake?"

"That is possible," said his lordship. "If she did, she may have been the one who drove her husband to Paraguay."

"And drove Sir James a little mad, too, I think," said the cabinet minister. "I have told you he was attractive to women, but women never interested him. Only a man deeply hurt in his past could have been quite so blind to their charms."

"Sir James, as he described himself, had become a hunter," said his lordship. "He was seeking what could not be found. If you read *The Descent of Ishtar*, you will see there the work of a Byron, worshiping his woman in stone."

"Never mind all that," said the inspector. "What I want to know is what your lordship has learned about what happened in Paraguay."

"I do not know the whole story," said his lordship. "All I can tell you is that there were two Englishmen, Graham Hart and a Mr. Evander Poole. One was killed under mysterious circumstances related to an explosion in a mine. The survivor, authorities believed, was the other man, Evander Poole. But this Poole then escaped over mountains and went into the country of Brazil."

"Are you saying," I asked, "that Graham Hart had changed places with him?"

"That is exactly what I am saying," said his lordship. "Graham Hart had become Evander Poole."

"And he came here," said the cabinet minister. "That seems to be something else you believe, since I heard you say that the murderer of Sir James would be someone the people here knew."

"Not everyone knew him," said his lordship, "but there were many who did."

"Did I know him?" Sam Shakespeare asked.

"You most certainly did," said his lordship. "Almost everyone at the table here knew him, except our guests who have come from London and also the inspector, of course."

"Of course," Inspector Bland repeated. "Is your lordship telling us this man came to town, put poison in his brother's wine bottle, and then simply vanished again?"

"Not at all," said Lord Tigraines. "You see, when the people here met Sir James, it was not really Sir James they were meeting. The man who came here was his brother. Graham Hart was the one we thought was Sir James."

Thirty

*C*ontrary to the custom in England, none of the ladies, now that the meal had been finished, had yet excused herself from the room; and so his lordship, rising from the table, made the suggestion that everyone should adjourn to the more comfortable Ferney salon. "I know," he said, "that some of the gentlemen will be anxious to light cigars, and I hope the ladies will be tolerant of that if they decide to join us."

We all got up; and though Fred Quint at first seemed to think he should stay behind, Lord Tigraines was especially insistent that he accompany us. "In what follows," his lordship told him, "your testimony will be of importance."

"My testimony?" asked Fred.

Fred seemed baffled, as indeed we all were, including the man from Scotland Yard. Inspector Bland, who only moments before had seemed to think he could make a joke of his lordship, now appeared to be in a state of shock. The truth is that I had begun to feel sorry for this man who had suddenly fallen from the heights of professional confidence. Sitting at the table with the cabinet minister, he must have seen a chance not only for promotion, but for future honors and fame. Now he staggered, as if walking in dreams. "Come, my good man," said the cabinet minister, placing a politician's hand on his shoulder. "I was as fooled by all this as you were, and you will find I am also like you in playing the gentleman's game. No word will cross my lips about it. It will be like a secret of state."

Once we were in the salon, his lordship, though not a smoker himself, handed out cigars to the men. The ladies were offered cigarettes, but only Lady Catherine took one. "I am sure you all still have questions," said his lordship. "The case is by no means complete. But I thought I would begin by explaining how it was that I first became suspicious of the man who called himself Sir James Hart. I am sure others shared my suspicions; and had the inspector been here to meet him, he would doubtless have pulled the mask off at once. As a matter of fact, it was my secretary, George Howard, who provided the first clue. George went to Redland to extend to Sir James an invitation to our New Year's banquet. At Redland he was met by two dogs that prevented his getting out of the car. Then the man who called himself Sir James appeared, and according to what George told me later, the man did not know who I was. All he said was something to the effect that I must have been the lord of the local manor."

"That was typical of Sir James, I would think," said the cabinet minister.

"Not if it was meant seriously," said his lordship. "I try not to be a prideful man. I realize, as the inspector has said, that I am only a person of leisure and of no consequence in the world. Nevertheless my leisure has allowed me to engage in a number of pursuits not unrelated to those of Sir James. At the least what I would have expected would have been some sort of accusation that I was a mere dilettante. But I do not want to dwell on myself, since I am sure that my experience in these things was paralleled by what others would have. Mr. Halliday, a most learned man, must also have detected something."

"I did detect something along those lines," said the vicar.

"I made the suggestion to him that he might like to give a lecture in the church. But he had no interest in that."

"I am sure not," said his lordship, "and if it is true that you were the one to whom he was writing the letter, that provides more evidence. If he did not want to continue the friendship, was it really because the two of you were on different paths? Or was it that you, with your knowledge, were in a position to expose him as false?"

"I understand and am relieved," said the vicar. "I could never see what he meant by that letter, or what it was, since I had tried to befriend him, that I might have said to offend."

"You need not worry on that score," said his lordship. "You did your duty as a Christian, and it was only the virtue of your knowledge that was to frighten him off."

"You are far too kind to me," said the vicar.

"Not at all," said Lord Tigraines. "But there is also Mr. Martree. One of the reasons I was pleased he could come was that he may have noticed things, too. The false Sir James came to his store."

"He came to the store twice," said Mr. Martree. "I asked if he would sign his name to his books, and he refused to do so. He seemed to think all I wanted was money and was going to charge more for them."

"Were you going to charge more?" asked his lordship.

"A little," Mr. Martree admitted. "I might have charged a few pennies more."

"The real Sir James might not have minded," said his lordship. "Who denies the profit of a few pennies to a man who is a seller of books, a dealer in what in our world is the only link between the words of the past and the minds of those who come in the future? Sir James was a worshiper of the past. He spent his life digging into the ground in order to expand what is known of the ancient civilizations. But his brother dug into the ground for profit. His work was only in the mines."

The inspector, though still hesitant, was at last ready to

speak again. "Excuse me, Lord Tigraines," he said, "but there is something I might add to this. Another reason he might not have wanted to sign the books is that the signature would not have been right. Such a forgery could be detected."

"Thank you, Inspector," said his lordship. "That is an important point, and when the writing in the unfinished letter is compared to that in the journal, we may have an additional proof."

"This is all very impressive," said Lady Catherine, "but I think something has been overlooked. If the man here was not the real Sir James Hart, what was it that had happened to him?"

"Why not let the inspector explain that?" said Lord Tigraines. "He has been patient in listening to me, and now I would like to listen to him."

"I believe," the inspector responded, "that your lordship should be allowed to continue. I do not feel, from the professional point of view, that I should commit myself at this time to something not fully investigated."

"You are undoubtedly wise in that," said his lordship, "and perhaps I should proceed with care, too. The outlines of the situation are clear, but not all the facts are yet known. Please be ready to correct me, Inspector, if you feel my conclusions are wrong."

"I will be happy to," the inspector said.

"Good," said his lordship. "Then let us see where we are. Assuming that what has been said so far is true, and that Graham Hart left Paraguay for Brazil, we must try to imagine his state of mind. Tortured by the fame of his brother, and driven mad by his wife, did he roam the jungles of Brazil with the thought of taking revenge? He was Cain, as the inspector has described him, and his brother was the gifted Abel. One might even be led to surmise that when he took on the identity of a dead man, his former friend Evander Poole, the seed of thought had already been planted that he could change places again. Here, though, we encounter a problem, which is not merely one of motive, but of human nature itself. Just as the ancient Pittacus has told us that virtue is hard, so also is its opposite. True evil does not exist."

It was typical of Lord Tigraines to elevate the discussion like this, and nothing could better demonstrate the superiority of his reasoning than the exchange that followed.

"What of Jack the Ripper?" asked the cabinet minister. "Are you saying he should not be called evil?"

"In his actions he was evil," said his lordship, "but we do not know what he was in his mind. He may have thought he was an agent of the Almighty. History gives us examples of this in its many religious wars, persecutions, and misguided idealists. For all we know, when Graham Hart sought out his brother, he may have hoped they at last could be friends. With the money he had earned or stolen, he may even have become rich."

"But where did they meet?" asked Lady Catherine.

"There is uncertainty about that," answered his lordship. "It is possible that they met in Baghdad or in the hills where Sir James was then held. Sir James, for the second time, had been kidnapped, and his brother, like our friend here before, was the one who ransomed him."

"That is extraordinary," said the cabinet minister. "Do you mean this brother went all the way to Baghdad to ransom his worst enemy?"

"We do not know why he went there," said his lordship. "We know only that this was done, after which both Sir James and his brother boarded a ship for England. Naturally, no one knew they were brothers, since one used the name Evander Poole. But the two were to share the same lifeboat when the ship sank in a storm."

"And then what happened?" asked the cabinet minister.

"One of them drowned," said his lordship, "and the other nearly lost his life, too. You could say the death was accidental, or that Sir James was a victim of the sea; but I do not think so myself. I believe that when they were out in that boat the boyhood rivalry was renewed. Not only, as we look to the past, should we think of them as Cain and Abel. Even more they were Set and Osiris, the brother gods of the Egyptians. Those gods, too, both loved the same woman, the goddess Isis who was their sister."

"Osiris was drowned," I said.

"That is right," said his lordship. "After Osiris returned from his journey civilizing the world, Set had a beautiful chest measured to Osiris' size. At a banquet this chest was presented; and when Osiris had lain down inside, Set had it closed, its lid fastened, and then thrown into the Nile. The chest drifted until it washed up on the distant Phoenician shore."

"Did the body of Sir James wash up somewhere?" I asked.

"Only his journal was found," said his lordship. "But the journal was in the arms of his brother, which was why doctors and others made the mistake that they did."

Thirty-one

*L*ord Tigraines, as usual, had been careful to stay within the bounds of what was known. He could not, and therefore he did not, say with certainty what had occurred. It was our imaginations, each of them different, that painted in the rest of the scene, as those brothers, enemies since boyhood, felt passions rise with the storm. "No wonder," Sam Shakespeare said, "the man told Susan he believed in reincarnation. He was a living example of it."

"But only partly," said his lordship. "Even while he was still there in France, where he had been pulled from the sea, he was seen by someone else from the ship who reported him as Evander Poole. Before the false Sir James came here to England, the French almost discovered the truth. And here, too, he would have problems. He may have thought he would be reaping the harvest of his brother's celebrity, but neither the fine clothes he wore to our banquet nor the beard on his face could hide the difference in the two minds. Mr. Martree, as I understand it, once made the suggestion to him that Ishtar, on whom Sir James was an expert, may have been thought to take the form of a star, or of a meteor falling to earth. Yet not even this made an impression. No, the man was living with risk, which would be with him until the day of his death."

"Now," said the cabinet minister, "you have mentioned something I have been thinking of, too, and that is the death of this impostor himself. That part of the case is not solved."

"But the inspector has solved it," said the vicar. "He has told us it was a suicide."

"Yes," said the inspector, "that seems clear. Now that the question of identity is disposed of, I feel even more certain that my original solution was right. As his lordship has conceded, I did not have the opportunity others did to meet this Graham Hart in person and thereby detect him as false. When I spoke of suicide, therefore, I was speaking only of the death that occurred here. Whether it was the death of Sir James or of his brother has no bearing on its actual cause. Cause is what we investigate at the Yard. We assemble facts leading to a conclusion, and then we report that conclusion as proved."

"Has the conclusion been proven then?" asked his lordship.

"I do not yet have all the reports," answered the inspector, "that will soon be coming in on this case, but it is not hard to see that a man who has killed his own brother has already killed a part of himself. Conscience may not be a word that is familiar to everyone here, but it is what we in the Yard call the policeman of the soul. A man in the grip of his conscience does not need handcuffs or bars. If he is like this man you knew in Marley, he does not even need a hangman. Some believe suicide cheats the hangman, but I see it, as the vicar may, too, as the sentence of a different tribunal."

"It is a pleasure to hear this," said the vicar, "from a man who is in your walk of life. I did not realize that under their badges the police would be wearing my cloth. Naturally, we cannot celebrate the act of someone's taking his own life. Too often it results not from conscience, but from the tragedy of despair. There is, though, as you say, a tribunal above any here on the earth, and the final weighing belongs to it. Let us hope this Graham Hart, through his death, will receive some ultimate forgiveness for the things that he did in his life." The vicar turned to his lordship. "Do you not agree with me, Lord Alfred?" he asked.

"Indeed I do," said Lord Tigraines. "I have never found punishment a good teacher, and I am sure this tribunal you speak of, with its wisdom of eternity, long ago devised some other method for dealing with our people on earth. But I am still in doubt about a number of points related to this particular case. Though we know that the wine had been poisoned, we do not know where the poison came from. Have any efforts been made to trace it?"

"We looked everywhere," the constable said. "We got down on our hands and knees and went over every inch of the house, not just downstairs but all over it. I had already searched it myself; but after the inspector arrived, he made me start at the beginning with him."

"And what about the stores?" asked his lordship. "Was an effort made to trace the poison through them?"

"Of course there was," said the inspector. "That was one of the first things I did. Every chemist's shop in the area was visited and its records subjected to the most careful examination. There had been a number of purchases of poisons, and if the death had been by prussic acid or strychnine, I might well have had a list of suspects. But arsenic, as was used in this case, had not been purchased near here. The only conclusion, therefore, is that Mr. Hart—I almost said Sir James—had purchased the poison elsewhere. He carried it with him, in the wine, always ready for the time when he would put an end to himself."

"What kind of wine was it?" asked his lordship.

"That," said the inspector, "could not be determined because the label had been removed from the bottle. As everyone knows, the best wines often come from Portugal; but whether it was of that type, or was something Mr. Hart brought from France, it is now too late to tell. These questions your lordship asks are dead ends. They have all been fully explored through our normal methods of inquiry. Of course, if your lordship has interest in visiting the scene of crime, I know that Sir Bruce Nottingham would want that courtesy extended not only to your lordship, but also to your lordship's guests. We could go there at this very moment, should people wish to have my statements confirmed."

"It is a little late to go there now," said his lordship. "I am sure our guests would not want to be troubled by any such excursion as that."

"I would not be troubled," said the cabinet minister. "As a matter of fact, after all this discussion and the doubts cast on his reasoning, I think we owe it to the inspector to let him show us his methods of work. Perhaps Mr. Halliday would prefer not to come. I can understand that a man of his calling—"

"Would be most anxious," the vicar said. "If others go, I will want to go with them. The ladies, though—"

"They will come," said Lady Catherine. "We are left out too much as it is."

As several others started speaking at once, and all of them with similar protests, his lordship got up from his chair. "George," he said, "you had better get the lanterns since there may be no lights in the house. I had been planning to end this discussion by letting Fred Quint explain what he knows, but if everyone wishes to go to Redland, he will be able to do it there."

"Mr. Quint, you say?" asked the inspector.

"Yes," said his lordship, "but let us go now before it gets any later. I will, now that I think about it, be very interested to see this house that the police have searched so thoroughly."

Thirty-two

*N*aturally, it would have been my wish to travel in the car with his lordship; but he had already been joined by Susan and her husband, the two guests, and then Fred Quint in front, even before the inspector started insisting that he wanted to sit at Fred's side. After thanking the vicar and his wife for offering to let me ride with them, I got into the Shakespeares' car with Mr. Martree.

Sam had a little trouble with the crank, which meant the others got a head start; but we soon felt the wind in our faces as Sam pressed the pedal to the floor. The headlights, probing into the dark, revealed a night filled with insects, invisible or sleeping by day, that traveled together in clouds. After we passed, some of them were still glowing, and looked like dust between stars.

Perhaps the others did not see this, however; for none of them mentioned it. Until Mr. Martree began speaking, only the noise of the engine broke the silence of the night. "I count this day," said Mr. Martree, "as the most wonderful one of my life. I never thought when I came to this town, a poor clerk opening his own store, that I would find myself at a table not only with Lord Tigraines, but with his grace and all you other people. I am not, of course, a Dr. Johnson, but I know now how he must have felt when the king came into the library, surprising him there at the fire."

At that moment we were passing through town; and on the left, with a street lamp shining on it, was the little Martree Bookstore, not so different, perhaps, from the one where the young Samuel Johnson grew up with blind eyes reading books. The Green Fox, a block ahead on the right, had no one standing outside it this evening, though from within laughter could be heard, followed by three notes on the piano. Someone may have been about to sing.

Sam stopped the car in his own driveway, and we walked to Redland through the trees, a shortcut with the moon in the branches and the lanterns helping find the old wall. That wall, crumbling like the high chimneys, had a place where we could climb over it, among the bits of broken mortar and brick. "This spot bothered me once," said Sam Shakespeare, as Amanda, who had been a sportswoman, reached back to give him a hand. "In those days when that man had those dogs here, I wanted to brick it back up."

The others were already waiting by the time we reached the house, where one of the lanterns was given to the inspector and the other to Lord Tigraines. Then the inspector, after removing the seal that had been keeping the curious out, opened the way to a hall in which tables were turned on their sides, chairs stacked about, and lamps and pictures left in a pile on the floor. For a moment, as I first entered it, the house looked for all the world like a tomb that I had seen opened in Egypt, and where some ancient and brave band of robbers, themselves suddenly trapped inside, had disturbed the room of sleep of a Pharaoh.

"Well, Inspector," said his lordship, "you and Ravenwood have certainly done your work."

"It was necessary," the inspector answered. "We had to make sure we searched everything. Of course, when the house has new tenants, the constable can help straighten things up.

But here you see a very good example of what I call thoroughness. Everything here is a piece in the puzzle and has helped in my solving the case."

"Do these pieces fit then?" asked his lordship.

"No," said the inspector, "they do not. No pattern in them was discovered, and no pattern ever will be. But now I would like to turn your attention to the stairs and to the place where the body was found. The body was exactly seven steps from the top, which indicates, if the man was on his way down, that the poison did its work very quickly."

"Where did he drink the poison?" asked his lordship.

"That is something else," said the inspector, "that cannot now be determined. The only glasses and cups that were found were the ones in the kitchen, but they could have been taken back there from some other place in the house."

"The man would have been in great pain," said the doctor, "and not only with a thirst, but with an acute nausea. I would say that the poison was most likely consumed in the kitchen and that the victim was on his way up the stairs. I also think, when he collapsed, he was writhing. As I said at the inquest, his face had the look of the plague."

"In that case," said the cabinet minister, "his crimes were all paid for right then."

"What do you think, Timothy?" asked his lordship. "You lived here in the house with the man. Do you think his crimes were paid for?"

"I do not know," Timothy answered. "When I come into this house and see all the furniture thrown about, I think about the man I used to see sitting every night by himself in that chair that is now upside down. I heard what was said during dinner, and I know his brother drowned at sea. I also know the man was not what I thought, and that his mind, when he sat in that chair, was not thinking what I thought it was then. He was not the great Sir James Hart, whose work I heard about back in school. He was not the one who dug up all the tablets with the offerings to Ishtar on them. But to me, you see, he was that man. And to me, in spite of all of these theories, he really still is Sir James."

"That was well spoken," said his lordship, "and you are to be commended for it. But now let me ask something else, since I am not yet clear on one point. Your wife Susan was sick, we have heard. Is it possible that Graham Hart also might have been ill?"

"Oh, yes," said Timothy, "he was coming down with a cold. It was difficult for him to talk that night."

"Even that night then," said his lordship, "the very night that he died, you yourself had a conversation with him."

"We often talked," Timothy said. "He knew I was trying to be an actor, and he did say something once that might, when I look back on it, be related to his being an impostor. I am afraid, though, that if I repeat it, some people here might be offended."

"We are all here at our risks," said his lordship, "and offense is one of those we must take. Go on. It could well be important."

Nonetheless, Timothy paused before replying: "I was talking to him about actors and about all the costumes we wear, changing them behind screens and curtains in time to be in the next scene. Then he said: 'That is the only difference between an actor on the stage and in life. In life we keep on our costumes.'"

"That does not seem particularly offensive," said the cabinet minister. "Was that all, or did he go on from there? Possibly did he give you examples?"

"Yes," said Timothy, "he mentioned a number of people who he said were just actors dressed up, saying lines they were expected to say."

"I suppose he mentioned me," said the vicar.

"People in professions were mentioned," said Timothy. "It was his opinion that a policeman, for example, could equally well be a doctor, a dogcatcher, or if your lordship will accept my pardon, a lord."

"He got you with that one, Tigraines," said the cabinet minister. "He reached out of the grave and got you."

"And I think he got me, too," said the vicar. "Are you sure I was never included in any of these things that he said?"

"He mentioned vicars, yes," said Timothy, "but I am sure that he could not have meant you. What he said, you see, was that the world was the setting for a great masquerade."

"We can accept that, I think," said his lordship, with a glance at the cabinet minister. "I have often had the same thought myself. But was this what he talked about on the night that was to be the last of his life?"

"No," said Timothy, "he barely spoke then. He had the start of a cold, as I said. But after supper he did say that I should go to see how Susan was."

"And did you do that?" asked his lordship.

"Yes," said Timothy.

"That was a little dangerous, was it not," said his lordship, "since the police were then looking for you?"

"I was careful," Timothy explained. "I took the back streets, and then I climbed to Susan's window on the trellis at the back of the house. But Sir James, or the man I thought was Sir James, always said that if I was arrested he would hire Mr. Shakespeare to defend me. You see, I think before I came he was lonely, and that was why he wanted me here."

"Then let us make sure this is understood," said his lordship. "On the night that the man drank the poison you were not here in this house."

"No," said Timothy, "not until almost morning."

"Then that was why, even if he cried out," said Lord Tigraines, "you would not have been able to hear him."

"Yes," said the young man, his head lowered and his hand clutched in his wife's.

Thirty-three

*I*nspector Bland, for the last several minutes, had not seemed to be following the discussion, but had returned to his scrutiny of Fred Quint. First he would shift to one side, and then, along with all the shadows cast by the lantern he held, he would move behind the man's back. The inspector's face, so calm when I first saw it, had seemed since to age twenty years. In his eyes a gleam of madness was shining, while all the time Fred Quint himself merely smiled benignly at his daughter and at those hands joined in love.

"Did you hear that, Inspector Bland?" asked his lordship. "Timothy was not here on that night. Graham Hart was in the house alone."

"I did not need to hear," said the inspector. "I know that, and I also know what your lordship is attempting to prove. Once it has been established that the victim was alone in the house, we will know why no one saw his assassin. Your lordship worked here while I was in London, just as your lordship worked in London while I was here. It may seem to the rest of the world that your lordship's interests are up in the clouds. But I know better. I have been a detective far too long to be fooled."

"No one wishes to fool you," said his lordship. "This case is all we want to solve. You are right that I did work in London, though unfortunately it was cut short. And you are also right that I have done some work here. This very morning, while you were in court, a kind of experiment was performed."

"An experiment with poisons?" asked the detective.

"No," said his lordship, "we will get to that later. This experiment had to do with the screams that the Shakespeares once heard in the night. They are the closest neighbors to Redland, and those screams, it was suggested, could have come from a Gramophone. I understand, too, that there is one in this house."

"It was one of the first things I found," said the inspector. "It was hidden in a closet upstairs."

"Yes," said his lordship, "and so when George went to London, I had him purchase one for my niece. We had a chance to listen to it this morning, just to test out the way it would sound. You may have done that, too, inspector; but what I would like to ask now is if anyone who was out in the garden thought the singer was there in the house."

"I did not," said Lady Catherine, "but then I have heard Caruso before."

"And that is not all," continued his lordship. "If one is listening to a recording, music will also be heard. The sound of instruments, on occasion, will become just as loud as the voice. Thus I think we can be sure that it was not a Gramophone that was heard."

"Some people must think our minds are slow," said the inspector, moving back behind Fred Quint again. "I know what this is leading up to. There is a suspect; but before he is presented, your lordship wants to go back through the case and refute all the old evidence. Your lordship does not need to do that. Once again all we want is a name; therefore, in spite of my better instincts and the conclusions I had previously reached, I must ask that everyone remains still. No one is to move from this room or to reach down and touch anything. I am not armed, but I have this lantern, which I can easily crack on a head. Now go on, Lord Tigraines. Is this suspect a relative of the girl who worked here? Is it her father, who as a gardener would undoubtedly have access to poisons, and who, in a fatherly rage, did away with his daughter's employer?"

Not only, with his lantern held high, had the inspector moved behind the suspect, but the constable, ignoring the injunction that everyone should remain still, circled over to the inspector's side.

"Good grief," his lordship said, "of course not. How could I ever suspect that Susan's father would have done such a thing? I have known the man since my boyhood, when he dressed as he is dressing today. He was a butler, and a very fine one; but he preferred, after the death of his wife, to work outside in the garden. I need not tell you that death often brings change, and in Fred it brought a love of nature and a sense of comfort, as I think he might say, in the sight of the renewal of life. No, Inspector, my gardener does not use poisons. A poison might kill a rodent or insect, but they are part of nature themselves. Each creature has a right to creation, and to live out its life in its own way."

"Yes," said the inspector, "we know that. But your lordship said there was to be testimony. Your lordship told us more than once at Longmoor that Mr. Quint would have something to say."

"He does, and he will say it," said his lordship, "just as soon as everything is prepared. A fine speaker like Mr. Quint deserves to have a proper introduction."

"Then is there no suspect?" asked the inspector.

"Not a suspect at all," said his lordship. "What I have is a near certainty. If all you ask is to be given a name, I will give you the name Norma Hart. You have told us you believe Graham Hart died as a result of suicide. I believe that at least the poison was something put there by his wife."

"But you need evidence," said the cabinet minister. "What proof do you even have she was here?"

"First there were the screams," said his lordship, "and then there was also the Gramophone. It was in a closet, as the inspector has told us, which must mean that Graham Hart did not use it. Someone else may have used it, however; and I believe that person was his wife, who was also the owner of the dogs."

"The dogs?" said the cabinet minister. "What could possibly make you think that?"

"They were not puppies," answered his lordship. "Redland's master had not bought them here, nor did he have them with him in France. There is a woman whom George talked to in London and who had seen this Norma some years ago. Later she saw her from the top of a bus, when unfortunately she was two blocks away. I asked George if the woman had told him whether Norma was alone, but George said he had not asked that. Had he asked, and had the woman said that Norma was walking those dogs, we would have more certain proof. As it is, the main thing to consider is the peculiar way they behaved. With the exceptions of Graham Hart himself and the inspector, who was able to take them in hand, those dogs would attack men, but not women."

"That is right," Susan said. "They liked me. I could reach down and take their collars, and they purred at me just like kittens."

"But they could also be vicious," said his lordship, "and that viciousness may have been a reflection of the way their mistress felt toward the world. The woman in London said that she was a witch."

"I feel sorry for her," said Lady Catherine. "From what you say, she must have had a hard life. Torn between those two brothers, it was as if she were under a curse."

"When Graham Hart came back from France," said his lordship, "newspapers said that he was Sir James. The poor woman, who had married the wrong brother, may have thought, before they met again, that she and Sir James would be together at last. Instead, she found only deception. It was

Graham, not Sir James, returning, and she must have known what that meant."

"So she poisoned him," said Lady Catherine.

"Her husband drank the wine, yes," said his lordship. "It appears that after Susan got sick, and after he, too, came down with a cold, he may have at first heated a cup, which he was taking as a medicine. But then, with the thirst from the poison, he drank the whole bottle at once."

"That means I was the one who killed him," said Susan. "I killed him when I gave him the cold."

"Your cold was an instrument," said his lordship, "but there were other engines at work."

"What sort of engines?" asked the inspector.

"That we will see," Lord Tigraines said.

"Well, they will not be seen here," said the inspector, "or at least not if your lordship thinks that this house has a secret that is still undiscovered. I will grant that what your lordship has said has altered my opinions a little, but it has not changed the facts. Facts are what we at the Yard must rely on. No theory, no matter how plausible, can be considered of use without them."

"Nor would I suggest that it should," said his lordship. "With these lanterns we cannot see everything, but not everything has to be seen. In which direction is the kitchen?"

"Through that door and on the other side of the pantry," said the constable as he started that way. "I can assure your lordship, of course, that everything in the kitchen has been searched, but there is no harm in looking again."

"No, indeed," said the inspector. "I welcome Lord Tigraines' searching it, since that may teach his lordship respect for the work we police do ourselves."

We left that place where the lanterns had cast eerie shapes on the walls, and where the stairs and stacked furniture had breathed out the odors of death. After filing through the narrow pantry, made even more narrow by all the drawers pulled out and blocking the way, we gathered in a single group in the kitchen. "This must be the table," said his lordship, "where Susan found the empty wine bottle. I see it has been wiped of all stains except those that are deep in the wood."

"Everything was wiped clean," said the inspector. "This was unwise and would not have been my instructions, but the death, as was said at the inquest, was not thought to be a murder at first."

"Nor even a suicide," the constable added. "I myself judged it a heart attack. Though I did not explain this before, I probably should have said at the inquest that I told Susan to go on cleaning things up. It seemed a way to occupy her attention while we waited for the doctor to come."

"Yes," said his lordship, "you tried to be thoughtful and cannot be blamed for that. In your searching you say you looked on the floor?"

"On our hands and knees," said the inspector.

"And what of the walls?" asked his lordship.

The inspector seemed about to throw up his hands. "The walls and cupboards were all searched," he said, "and not just here but all over the house. If your lordship thinks there might be secret panels, they have already been looked for, too."

"Right now," said Lord Tigraines, looking up, "I am thinking about the ceiling. It seems to me the poison might be there."

"Where?" asked the inspector

"There," said his lordship. "You can see it hanging down by that string."

"But that is flypaper," said the inspector.

"Yes, so it is," said his lordship. "It even looks as though it might be new, or at least purchased within the year."

"But it is there," said the inspector. "It is still there. That flypaper could not have poisoned the wine."

"Not that strip of it, no," said his lordship. "It serves only as an example to us to what Norma, too, may have seen. She may have stood here and watched the flies dying, which then told her what to do. That paper can be put into water. It can be boiled and with the gum separated, arsenic is what will remain."

"A witch's brew," said the cabinet minister. "Rather fitting for our Norma, I think, and for her Beelzebub."

"For the Lord of Flies, yes," said his lordship, "and for him more than one little strip might have been thought necessary. It was wise of the inspector to have made a search of those stores, but he should also have gone to the markets where such flypaper is sold. In such a place that kind of multiple purchase might still be remembered now."

Amanda Shakespeare nearly jumped in the air. "But I remember that myself," she said. "There was a woman in the market one day who bought five—no, I think it was six. I remember thinking then it was strange, though no stranger than the woman herself."

"By any chance," I said to her, "did this woman look like a witch?"

"She did have a screeching voice," said Amanda, "but she was not like a witch in a story. No, I think if I were a man I might even have found her attractive. But there was a sorrow—really an awful grief—that gave a strange cast to her features. Her eyes—I will never forget them. They were so deep and dark that it was as if they could see right through you."

Thirty-four

The confusion that reigned after this statement was something that I can hardly describe. All the ladies, with the exception of Lady Catherine, appeared also to have seen the woman in town. Mrs. Ravenwood had even spoken to her. And then, of course, when the husbands heard this, they wanted to know why they had not been informed. The constable seemed on the verge of a fit, stopping only when Lady Catherine began to say that she had seen a woman in London whose face was exactly the same. "I saw her," said Lady Catherine, "in a box at the opera last year."

"Impossible," said the cabinet minister.

"No, it is not," said the lady. "She looked right at me, and I had the most shuddering feeling. I thought then that I was about to die."

"We are all going to die," said the cabinet minister. "That is nothing that should concern us here. The only thing of importance at this moment is that this woman not be allowed to go free. I know that Inspector Bland has had trouble with other aspects of the case, but for the most part this was due, I am sure, to the fact that events had occurred that were outside of his jurisdiction. Now at last, since the vicar's tribunal may be too slow in its work, we have a case for Scotland Yard. It is the kind of thing our Yard people are good at. Believe me, they will track down this woman and get a confession from her."

"That should not be necessary or even possible," said his lordship. "The tribunal's work has been done."

"What are you saying?" asked the vicar.

"I am saying she is dead," said his lordship. "Her husband may have died from her wine, but she herself was dead months before that."

"Good Lord," said the cabinet minister, "do you mean to say he murdered his own wife?"

"He must have felt he had no choice," said his lordship. "After all, if she knew what had happened, he was not safe as long as she lived."

"Those screams we heard," said Amanda Shakespeare. "That must have been when he was killing her."

"I am sorry if you are shocked by that," said his lordship. "When the inspector suggested that we come to this house, I welcomed it, but also felt a reluctance, in view of what was going to be found. What I thought was that Fred Quint's testimony would be better heard at Longmoor. There, in cushioned chairs, you could listen without feeling everything was so close."

"Wait," said Inspector Bland. "Stop right there. I know what Lord Tigraines is going to say, and I want to assure everyone here that all this has been investigated. The possibility of an earlier murder, and even that a corpse could be found, has been given the fullest scrutiny. Outside, if people look in the garden, it will be seen there is a patch of loose dirt, where only now grass is starting to grow. I dug into that dirt with these hands, scratching all the way down to the point where it was clear that the earth was compacted and had not been disturbed before. There is no more chance of finding a body there than within the walls of this house."

"Yes," said his lordship, "you are right, I am sure. I am not suggesting that we dig there again. Please let Fred Quint explain what I told him, and how, once George Howard had assured me that the dogs would no longer be here, I sent Fred to examine the grounds."

"His lordship did send me here," said Fred Quint, at last having the chance to speak. "His lordship said that Mr. Howard had been told by Mr. Martree that Mr. Hart, who we thought was Sir James, had taken an interest in gardening. Now, of course I had been to Redland before. His lordship has often in the past allowed me to offer services to the smaller landowners in town. In particular his lordship was anxious to have me come here after the previous tragic death of Redland's owner who struck his head on a rock. Mr. Howard, too, accompanied me then, and we made a survey of the grounds."

"We are not interested in that," said the inspector. "We know that a previous owner fell and struck his head on a rock, but that was entirely accidental. A full record of that whole incident can be found in our files at the Yard. The man was drunk, but he was not drinking poison, and his blood, which was fresh on the stone, had no unknown footprints around it. As I recall, the only footprints discovered were his own and the constable's here."

"Yes," said his lordship, "but please let Fred continue. His purpose in mentioning that case was to explain exactly when he was here the first time and that Mr. Howard will be his witness."

"All right," the inspector said, "he can continue, but I do not see why your lordship thinks that a gardener, or even a man like Mr. Howard, could have evidence the Yard has not thought of."

"You do not consult with gardeners then," asked his lordship, "in the course of your investigations?"

"Of course I do," said the inspector.

"Then consult with one now," said his lordship. "Fred, I am sure the inspector did not mean to insult you. Please go on and explain to these people about any changes you found on your second visit to Redland."

"I did notice," said Fred, with no hint in his voice that he resented having been interrupted, "that there was a change between my first visit and this one recently. His lordship told me that Mr. Hart bought a book that describes some of my own work at Longmoor, and even has a small picture of me. What his lordship wanted to know was if the owner of Redland had copied anything from that book, and particularly in the area of transplanting. One of the things the book mentions, you see, is an idea that was really his lordship's, but that the book's author ascribes to me. This has to do with problems that develop when a plant is not in the right place. Plants, as you know, have no feet. They have roots, but they need us to move them, and what has been found at Longmoor is that often a plant that is dying can be saved if it is moved somewhere else. A tree or sometimes just a shrub may be casting a shadow on it. And then, of course, there are variations in soil, as well as rocks that can choke off a root. Sometimes, too, when it comes to plants, their greatest enemy will be another plant, which moves in and takes up the moisture. We all know how grass is attacked by weeds, and one day when his lordship and I were inspecting one of the lawns, his lordship said it was like Waterloo, where the squares of Napoleon's army were under attack from all sides. 'Wellington won that time,' said his lordship, 'and it looks as if he is going to win again.' "

"Please, Mr. Quint," said the inspector. "His lordship's great wit is well known. There is no need for you to go on and describe the whole battle to us."

"On the contrary," said the cabinet minister, "patriotism itself demands that we learn at least who was the victor."

"The Wellington weeds," said Fred Quint. "That French grass had no place at Longmoor."

"Mr. Quint, you are not in court," said the inspector, "but if you were, and spoke like that from the box, the judge might well hold you in contempt. At the very least you would be instructed to answer the questions you are asked. Did you, on your second visit, find that your daughter's employer had changed the grounds in some way?"

"Yes," said Fred, "I most certainly did. I noticed that patch of loose ground you spoke of, and it seemed to me there had been bushes there. I thought that if my memory served correctly they had been one of the species of bay, though not, of course, the *Laurus nobilis* which grows so well at Longmoor. Those shrubs at Redland had been peculiarly stunted, and I thought at first they might have died. But then I found them on the other side of the house, where they were now flourishing."

"In other words," said the inspector, "when you discovered this transplanting, you also learned why the ground was dug up."

"Yes, that is what I found," said Fred Quint. "I do not know if Mr. Howard would like to add something to it, but he was occupied on other work for Lord Alfred and was not with me on the second visit."

"No," I told him, "I have nothing to add except that I remember those bushes, too, and I remember your making the suggestion that just such a transplanting might help."

"And not just with the plants," said his lordship. "It would also serve to conceal the place where digging had been done. I am not speaking of shallow digging, inspector, but of digging deep enough for a grave."

There was something almost infinitely tragic on the face of Inspector Bland then. He said nothing, but one could see in his eyes that the energy of their darting was spent. As he stared at the flypaper, it was as if in that reminder of death he saw the entrance to the dark, empty chasm that in life is always at our shoulders, and always looming ahead.

"Come, my man," said the cabinet minister. "It cannot be as bad as all that. What Lord Tigraines says is pure speculation. We do not know if anything will be there."

"Yes, we do," said the inspector. Then he turned, and still in a low voice, he addressed himself to the constable. "Get the shovels, Ravenwood," he said.

Thirty-five

*T*he digging, there under the moon, was complicated at first by the fact that although the line of shrubbery was long, the grave itself would be far shorter, taking up only a small part of it. I myself, as Ravenwood seemed to tire, made the suggestion that we do what is done in archaeological excavations. There, before shafts and trenches are dug, smaller samples of the earth will be taken as probes are made into the ground. We had equipment for this at Longmoor, since we had used it after Fred found the mole that had swallowed a little disc of the sun, indicating that the soldiers of Mithra had built an underground temple there. But as Fred and I started to the car in order to get this equipment, his lordship told us to try the cane that Dr. Simpson was then leaning on. The cane worked, and soon we had the outlines of the exact place to dig.

"Now stand back," the inspector said after that. "I am the workman here, and I will work. If Mr. Quint wants to save all this shrubbery, he can do it after I dig it up. But I will dig, and I am going to keep digging until this case comes to an end. I have never known anything like it. I have never, in all my time at the Yard, had to be stopped and checked at each turn. Lord Tigraines is the victor. It has been proved beyond a doubt I was wrong. But as I dig, I will be digging for justice. I will be digging for truth. That is all, in the end, that will matter—just the knowledge that we have found what is here."

The inspector, in that moment, was awesome. He had proved, with these words, his true worth; and as he started the digging, it seemed he was not just a man, but a great engine at work. His hands, though they soon would be blistered, did not pause until he came to that point where he took off his coat and his collar. His shirt was soaked with sweat, his hair rumpled. He had not only blisters, but blood on his fingers and palms.

"It may be fortunate, Inspector Bland," the cabinet minister said to him, "that you have eaten all that meat. I can see, through your shirt, you have muscles."

The inspector looked up through the darkness at this man who was befriending him. "The only trouble now, your grace," he said, "is that I did not have any tonight."

I could have told him myself, of course, that without it his strength would not wane, but if anything would be increased. It was then, though, deep under the earth, that his shovel struck the first of the bones. They were charred. She had been in the furnace before what remained was put here. Looking down into that chasm, as the inspector's lantern flickered out, I was reminded by the sight of that skull of what the great Schliemann had said when he uncovered the hidden tombs at Mycenae. Schliemann, as he told the whole world, had thought he saw the face of Agamemnon, leader of the armies at Troy. But what I saw was the face of someone greater. It was Ishtar herself who was there.

"What is that?" said his lordship, lowering the second lantern. "It looks as though there is some sort of marking on that flat stone by the skull."

The inspector, bending down, picked it up; and in the tremble of light from the lantern, he read the chiseled writing out loud: "Here lie the bones of Norma Hart, who was killed by the hand of her husband in December of 1913. She yearned for the dead, not the living. She knew what could never be told."

There was silence as if a prayer had been spoken, but it was broken by the call of a bird. Then Lord Tigraines said: "If he wrote that, there must still have been love between them. After it all, and even after the brother, they must at least have felt its pain. Yes, the drinking of the poison may look to us like murder now. But that may not have been why she prepared it, and the inspector may have been right after all."

"Right about what?" asked the inspector.

"About suicide," Lord Tigraines said. "When Norma was mixing the poison, it may have been something for both of them. Remember what was said of Tristan and Isolde, that when they drank Love they drank Death. Norma's poison, too, was a philter, and would join them with the one who was gone, the hated and beloved brother who sought what could not be found."

"Then do you think," asked the vicar, "that they all have what they wanted now? Has the tribunal given them that?"

"All we can say," said his lordship, "is that they quarreled, as the Shakespeares once heard. Norma died before her bottle was opened, so that it was left on a shelf. It remained there, still unopened, until her husband, as so many of us do, came down with a cold in the spring."

The inspector, limp from his efforts, crawled at last out of the grave; and a little dirt, at least for the moment, was sprinkled back over the bones. They had been charred like a meteorite, I thought then, just as in the sky over the chimneys there was a long streak of light. It was as it had been and always will be when Ishtar descends to the earth.

Afterword

*I*t was there that the narrative ended, my great-uncle apparently satisfied that nothing more would ever need to be said. Sometime later there was a note attached, though, and it was written in a quite different hand, no longer coded but with a clear, perfect script.

The note did not add anything to the crimes, nor to the solution of them; but it did mention a kind of coincidence. It said that on the following day, after the grave had been opened, there was an incident across the channel in Europe. For it was on that day, June 28th, that the Archduke Francis Ferdinand was shot, thereby starting the first of the World Wars.

Lady Catherine, the note sadly informs us, became a nurse in the war and was killed. Timothy Loft, who here is called Corporal Staughton, died somewhere outside Verdun. His widow Susan then went to France, too, where she acted in a musical play put on for the entertainment of troops. The name of the play is not given, nor is the name Susan used; but it is said that when she returned to England, she became what she always had dreamed. According to Lord Tigraines, she was the greatest lady of the stage.

As for the bones of Norma Hart, I visited them myself in the churchyard, where moss had grown over the grave and where they now lay by her husband's. There was nothing, no sign at all, that the graves were of anything more than a quiet and gentle English couple who, because of their devotion, had passed away very close to each other, first the wife and then the husband, with only one season between. Something else, even stranger, however, was that the name on the husband's grave had not been changed. According to the names on those gravestones, Norma had been laid to rest with the brother, for the name on the other stone was that of Sir James. But maybe that was because of the war.